FaK

H

EMILY GOES TO EXETER

EMILY GOES TO EXETER

Being the First Volume of the
Travelling Matchmaker

M.C. Beaton

CHIVERS

British Library Cataloguing in Publication Data available

This Large Print edition published by AudioGo Ltd, Bath, 2011.
Published by arrangement with Constable & Robinson Ltd

U.K. Hardcover ISBN 978 1 445 83778 9
U.K. Softcover ISBN 978 1 445 83779 6

Copyright © M.C. Beaton 1990

Printed and bound in Great Britain by
MPG Books Group Limited

1

Go call a coach, and let the man be call'd,
And let the man who calls it be the caller;
And to his calling let him nothing call,
But Coach, Coach, Coach! O for a Coach,
Ye Gods!

Henry Carey

Hannah Pym stood by the drawing-room window of Thornton Hall and waited for the stage-coach to go by.

Thornton Hall was a large square building, rather like a huge doll's house, with a drive that led down to the Kensington Road. There were no formal gardens or trees at the front, only lawns cropped short by sheep, with the arrow-straight drive running down to tall wrought-iron gates flanked by stone gateposts topped with stone eagles.

It was six o'clock on a winter's morning and a low moon was shining. During the night, the wind had blown a light fall of snow into scalloped shapes across the lawns.

Hannah tugged open one of the long windows which led out on to a shelf of a balcony guarded by a wrought-iron railing. She walked out, and listened.

Then she heard it, the thud of hooves, and hung on to the rail and peered down the drive.

1

'Here she comes,' she whispered.

And bowling along the Kensington Road came the stage-coach, the Flying Machine, pulled by six powerful horses. She felt that breathless excitement which the sight of the stage-coach always gave her and lifted her hand and waved. The groom raised the yard of tin and blew a merry salute. The passengers on the roof were clutching their hats. How loud the horses' hooves were on the hard ground. What speed! And then the stage-coach was gone, taking life and adventure away into the darkness and leaving behind the bleak winter scene.

Hannah gave a little sigh and stepped inside and closed the window behind her.

Time was, she thought, when she had been too busy and happy to need the excitement of watching the stage-coach go by. That was when the mistress, Mrs Clarence, had been in residence: pretty, frivolous Mrs Clarence, filling the house with parties and friends and flowers and colour and light. But Mrs Clarence had run off with a footman just after Hannah had achieved her life's ambition and been made housekeeper.

Then a sort of darkness had fallen, for Mr Clarence had gone into a gloomy decline. Half the rooms were locked up, half the servants were dismissed and poor Hannah felt she was presiding at a perpetual funeral. That was when she began to wait for the stage-coach to go by, needing the sight of all that motion and life to raise her spirits. And then at last, she found she was supervising the arrangements for a real funeral. Mr Clarence had died just after Christmas.

In that year of 1800, the stage-coaches were advertised as Flying Machines. To Hannah they stood for everything that was missing from her now dark and bleak life: adventure, other worlds, hope, life and laughter.

But she could remember happy times before Mrs Clarence had run away, oh, so long ago, when life had been busy and exciting. At the age of twelve, she had left her parents' home in Hammersmith and entered into service in Thornton Hall, the Clarences' residence. She had worked hard to become a kitchen maid, then a between-stairs maid, then chambermaid, then housemaid, then chief housemaid, and had finally been exalted to the position of housekeeper. There had been servants' parties, she remembered, especially at Christmas, when Mrs Clarence and her husband would descend to the servants' hall and Mrs Clarence would dance with the menservants and Mr Clarence with the maids.

Hannah left the drawing-room and went down to the kitchens and made tea. She had always risen early, being one of those rare people who need very little sleep. She liked being up before the other servants to enjoy a

3

little bit of peace and quiet on her own.

She was worried. She was forty-five, a great age, nearly old. It would be hard to find another position as housekeeper. In making the arrangements for the funeral and coping with the Clarence relatives who had descended like vultures, she had not had time to seek another post. She had only a little money saved. 'And that,' said Hannah Pym aloud, 'is your own fault.' Hannah could not help interfering in other people's lives. There had been money given to servant girls to help them get out of trouble, somewhere to go and stay until the babies were born. There had been money given to a footman to go to university and make a new start, for he had been a bright, sensitive lad, hopeless as a footman. There had been money—Hannah winced—given to that under-butler who had proposed marriage to her. He had said he would go and purchase a cottage with her savings and had never come back. But now she was older and wiser and could often see through people and, besides, there was no use regretting the past.

The relatives, who had mercifully left for a few days after the funeral, were ready to descend again for the reading of the will. Sir George Clarence, Mr Clarence's brother, would be there this time, thought Hannah, and there would be someone to take charge. Sir George had been abroad in the diplomatic service for a long time and had returned to England only recently. She remembered him vaguely as being a rather austere and cold man. She felt sure Mr Clarence would not have remembered her in his will, although she was the last of the old servants. Since Mrs Clarence had left, the house had become too gloomy to attract regular staff, and a bewildering variety of maids and footmen had come and gone. It had been years since there had been a butler, that job having been added to Hannah's by the seemingly uncaring Mr Clarence.

The morning was busy with preparations for the reading of the will. A cold collation was to be served to the relatives in the dining-room about two o'clock. At four, they would adjourn to the library, where Mr Entwhistle of Entwhistle, Barker & Timms would read the will.

For a short while it was heart-breakingly like old times, with fires in the rooms and bustle and hurry. Hannah in her black gown and with her keys at her waist went here and there, running her fingers over ledges to make sure there was not a trace of dust, plumping up cushions, checking coal scuttles to make sure they were full, filling cans with hot water, arranging flowers, and giving a final polish to the brass and steel of fenders. Then, with the one remaining footman and two housemaids beside her, she waited in the hall for the

5

arrival of the relatives.

First came Mrs Jessop, the late Mr Clarence's sister, a small, fussy woman with her thin and whining husband and their three children, all boys in their teens, and spoilt, in Hannah's opinion, beyond repair. Then there was a fluttering of cousins, spinster ladies, gossiping and complaining about the cold. Then Mr Clarence's other brother, Peter, a fat, jolly man with a ferocious laugh and a weakness for practical jokes, his wife, Freda, fat also, but languid and a professional invalid, and their seven children of various ages.

And then arrived Sir George Clarence. He was a tall, spare man in his fifties with white hair, a hawklike face, and piercing blue eyes. He was impeccably dressed in a blue swallowtail coat and darker blue knee-breeches with striped stockings and buckled shoes, the splendour of which was revealed when the footman relieved him of his many-caped greatcoat.

'How are you, Miss Pym?' he asked, and Hannah flushed with pleasure because he had remembered her name. She had never adopted the courtesy title of 'Mrs', like most housekeepers and cooks, and he had remembered that too.

She supervised the serving of the cold collation. Bedrooms had been prepared, although no one but Sir George was staying the night, because she knew the guests would like somewhere to retire.

Then when the ladies had gone through to the drawing-room and the men were left to their wine, she went down to the hall to greet the lawyer, Mr Entwhistle.

'Bitterly cold,' he said, rubbing his hands. 'There is more snow coming, I can feel it.'

'I have put a tray in the morning-room, sir,' said Hannah. 'I thought you might care for some refreshment before the reading of the will.'

'Most kind of you, most kind. But business first, I think. Miss Pym, the housekeeper, is it not?'

'Yes, sir.'

'Then you had better be present at the reading of the will. Lead the way, if you please.'

Hannah escorted him to the library before summoning the relatives. Her first elation was quickly dying down. Mr Entwhistle was a kindly old gentleman in a bagwig. His invitation to her to be present at the reading of the will was merely a courtesy. Why, poor Mr Clarence had barely noticed her existence in his final years.

Miss Pym bustled about, ordering the staff to find chairs for all the relatives and lighting lamps and candelabra, for the library was a dark room, the serried ranks of calf-bound books seeming to absorb what light there was.

She then took up a position by the door.

Mr Entwhistle took out spectacles from his spectacle case and polished them with maddening slowness. Hannah could feel the tension rising in the room. Only Sir George, sitting over by the window, appeared indifferent to the contents of the will. But then he would know the contents. Mr Clarence had told her a long time ago that he had appointed Sir George as his executor.

At last, Mr Entwhistle began. Thornton Hall, its grounds and all its contents were to be left to his dear brother, Sir George Clarence. There was a heightening rather than a lessening of tension as if everyone was privately asking, 'The money. What about the money?'

They were soon put out of their misery. The bulk of Mr Clarence's considerable fortune had been divided equally among his two brothers and one sister and then there were handsome legacies to every single one of the other relatives. Smiles all round, then a few sentimental tears shed by the spinster cousins—'So kind, so very, very kind of him to remember us all.'

'Now to the servants,' said Mr Entwhistle. Now the tension was in Hannah. 'To any servant in my employ for the period of over four years at my death I leave two hundred pounds each.'

Hannah felt quite limp with relief. That would keep her for long enough and more to find a job. There were not many servants who had lasted the four-year period, she reflected. The house had been so gloomy that servants came and went, not many of them staying long. But there was the coachman and the outside man, and one of the scullery maids, and the remaining footman. Then she heard her own name.

'To my faithful housekeeper, Miss Hannah Pym, I leave the sum of five thousand pounds to be hers entirely and to do with as she wishes.'

There were little rustles of irritation which gradually grew louder as Mr Entwhistle took off his glasses, polished them again, and put them carefully away in a leather case. Five thousand pounds! 'Too much for a servant!' said one of the cousins. 'She'll only drink it,' hissed another. But Hannah stood by the door in a happy daze. She would never need to work again. Automatically, she walked down the stairs to the morning-room to see that everything was laid out for Mr Entwhistle. Finally, she stood at the door to help the departing relatives on with their cloaks and mantles. Not one of them tipped her, considering she had more money than was good for her.

Hannah then returned to the library to see if Sir George required anything and was told he did not. She bustled about the bedrooms with the maids, seeing that the mess left by the

9

relatives had been cleared up. The bedchambers had been meant to be used only as places in which to freshen up, but they had all managed to make a horrendous mess just the same, the children having created a great deal of the havoc. Then downstairs to see the lawyer on his way. She longed to ask him how soon she could have the money but found she had not the courage. Her initial excitement was fading fast. She had a vague idea that wills could take forever, some slow legal process whereby the money was finally disgorged reluctantly when the recipients were nigh dead.

Hannah glanced at the watch she wore pinned to her bosom. Nearly six o'clock. Time for the stagecoach to go by.

Sir George went quietly into the drawing-room and stood watching the housekeeper as she stood by the window, one hand raised to hold back the curtain. The window was open and he heard the thud of horses' hooves and the blast of a horn. The housekeeper waved and then turned slowly round, her eyes full of dreams. She started slightly at the sight of him and turned back and closed the window.

'Are you expecting some friend or relative to arrive by stage-coach?' asked Sir George.

'No, sir,' said Hannah over her shoulder as she swung the heavy shutters across the window. 'I like to see the coach go by.'

She then began to move about the room,

10

lighting the lamps, poking the fire and throwing a log on it. He came and sat down in a chair by the fire. 'Sit down, Miss Pym,' he said.

Hannah looked at him in surprise. 'I do not think it would be right,' she said.

'You are now an heiress,' said Sir George, looking amused. 'Pray, take a chair.'

Hannah sat down gingerly on the very edge of a chair, facing him. He studied her for a few moments.

She was a thin woman with thick sandy hair under a starched cap. She had a sallow face with a crooked nose, slightly bent, and a long, humorous mouth. Her eyes were extraordinary, very large and bright, of many colours, it seemed, at times gold, at times blue, at times green. She had hunting shoulders although she did not know how to ride a horse, very square, and long thin arms and surprisingly elegant hands. Her ankles were very well turned. Hannah had automatically raised her skirt a little as she sat down. Her ankles and feet were her one vanity and she spent too much money on shoes.

'What will you do with your fortune?' asked Sir George. 'Buy a little cottage? Retire?'

She clasped her hands tightly and looked at him as a simply wonderful idea entered her mind.

'No, sir,' said Hannah. 'I shall travel. On the stage-coach.'

'Where?'

Hannah threw out her hands, her sallow face flushed with excitement, those odd eyes blazing. 'Anywhere.'

'For the sake of travel. How strange.'

'You see, sir,' said Hannah earnestly, 'I crave adventure.'

'A journey on a stage-coach, particularly in winter,' he said dryly, 'is full of adventure— broken traces, snow-drifts, mud, highwaymen, footpads, and damp beds in the wayside inns.'

'Yes, sir.' The housekeeper's odd eyes appeared to have lost all colour and become as bleak as the winter landscape outside.

'But if that is your wish . . .' he said quickly.

'It means much to you?'

'Oh, yes, sir.' The eyes flashed green. 'The Flying Machines, the excitement, the motion, the towns and cities. I shall travel to the ends of the earth.'

'Stage-coaches do not go to the ends of the earth,' he pointed out.

'I know. But all over England. Bath, York, Exeter. Life, adventure. . . and hope, sir.'

'How gloomy it must have been here for you,' he said sympathetically. 'Why not try one stage-coach journey and see how you fare?'

'I do not want to seem mercenary,' said Hannah. 'But. . . but, how soon can I have some money?'

'You can get an advance from Mr Entwhistle as soon as you like. I would advise

12

you to bank your fortune.' Hannah's face fell.

'Come now,' he said gently, 'you cannot travel the length and breadth of England with sacks of sovereigns.'

'It's just,' said Hannah, twisting her hands in her lap, 'that I do not know anything about banks.' She bit her lip, remembering the perfidy and cheating of that under-butler who had run off with her savings. 'What if, sir, the banker should prove a cheat and run off with my money?'

'Banks are not like that. Look, we shall go to the lawyer's together tomorrow—I have to see him about a few things—and we will get you an advance. Then I shall take you to my bank and they will explain to you about cheques and bank drafts and all such complications.'

'Sir, you are very good.'

'Think nothing of it, Miss Pym. Now, as to dinner, tell cook to supply a simple meal. Have the servants who have been here longer than four years been told of their two hundred pounds?'

'Yes, sir. Or rather, I told the footman and I assume he told everyone else.'

'As I shall be closing this place up, I think Mr Entwhistle should advance them the money now or it might be very difficult to find them after the estate is sold and everyone has dispersed to different parts of London.'

'Yes, sir,' said Harriet dutifully, although

she was sure that any servant with the expectation of two hundred pounds would not stay away from the lawyers for very long.

'That will be all.'

Hannah rose and curtsied and left. Her head was full of excitement and dreams. Where would she go first? Exeter, she thought. Instead of standing by the window watching the Flying Maching hurtle past, she would be on it herself!

* * *

At ten o'clock the following morning, Sir George sent for her and told her to make herself ready to go to the lawyers. He said he would meet her in the hall in half an hour.

Hannah ran to her room and wrenched off her black gown and cap. She was going out in the company of a gentleman and must look like a lady. She had one silk gown, a golden-brown colour. It was of old-fashioned cut with the waist being where a waist should be instead of up under the armpits as present fashion decreed. The day was bitterly cold. She hesitated and then ran up the stairs and through the long corridors to Mrs Clarence's old rooms, which had been kept locked up. Mrs Clarence had fled only in the clothes she stood up in. Her clothes, never touched since the day she had gone away, hung in two large wardrobes.

14

With a feeling of great daring, Hannah selected a dark-blue velvet cloak and then lifted down a beaver hat. She was sure Sir George would give them to charity. She would find the right moment to tell him she had borrowed them and ask if she might pay for them.

She carried them back down to her room and put hat and cloak on. She hoped she looked like a lady. She felt she did. But when she met Sir George, a grand figure in a many-caped coat and shining top-boots, she felt just like a servant in borrowed clothes.

He helped her into his carriage exactly as if she had been a lady and Hannah began to feel a little more assured.

The well-sprung carriage bowled down the drive. Hannah looked out eagerly, rubbing at the misted glass with her glove and pressing her crooked nose against the window.

'Miss Pym,' he said, 'it is like escorting a prisoner out of jail. Did you never leave the grounds?'

'Hardly ever, sir. There was so much to do, you see. When I was younger, I would sometimes go to the play—that was when Mrs Clarence was here, but not for a very long time now.'

'Have you no relatives? No friends?'

'Such friends as I had, sir, were among the staff,' said Hannah, 'but they gradually all found posts in other households. My family were all killed in the smallpox epidemic of ninety-two.'

'You were with the Clarences a long time?'

'I started as scullery maid at the age of twelve. They were newly married then, Mr and Mrs Clarence. I rose up the ranks and became housekeeper eighteen years later. But it was shortly after that that Mrs Clarence ran away. She would have been about thirty-five years then, sir, and the footman only twenty-five.' Hannah squinted down her nose in sudden embarrassment. He might consider it vulgar of her to regale him with such gossip.

Hannah turned her attention back to the moving scene outside. She was a gossip and knew it. Time after time, she had tried to stop her clacking tongue, and time after time it had got her into trouble. But not for ages. There had been no one really to talk to.

Hannah was very disappointed in the lawyer's office. It was dark and musty. Could do with a good scrub, thought Hannah with a sniff. She had somehow imagined that everywhere she went with Sir George would be grand and elegant. Mr Entwhistle gave her a bank draft for one hundred pounds. 'It is the same bank as mine,' said Sir George. 'We are going there now, Mr Entwhistle, to arrange an account for Miss Pym. Now, there are various other things I would like to discuss with you . . .'

Hannah drifted over to the window which

looked out on to Lincoln's Inn Fields. A fine snow was beginning to fall from the leaden sky. Then, as she watched, the flakes grew thicker, but still buoyant on a mischievous wind, scurrying in circles, swirling up to the window and spiralling down again. Five thousand pounds! The full impact of the legacy hit Hannah in all its glory. The spectre of the workhouse receded. She was a lady of independent means. She brushed the fine velvet of the cloak she wore with a complacent hand.

Sir George quickly completed his business and took Hannah to Child's Bank. The bank was every bit as grand as Hannah could wish, but instead of feeling happy and confident she began to feel diminished. A friend of Sir George's approached him while they were waiting for the bank manager. To Hannah's confusion, Sir George introduced her to his friend, a Mr Cadman. She was so used to being invisible to the Quality that she stammered and blushed. 'How goes the world?' Sir George asked Mr Cadman. 'Still gambling on everything and anything?'

'Had the most miserable run of luck at White's,' said Mr Cadman. 'Lost fifteen thousand guineas last night. But I shall come about.'

Hannah felt herself shrivelling. Here was a world in which gentlemen could lose such vast sums in one night. And she had thought five thousand pounds had raised her to the ranks of the gentry!

An usher came up and said the manager was ready to see them. Hannah's mercurial spirits went soaring up again like a balloon. For the manager treated her with deference and seemed to find nothing odd in the fact that she knew absolutely nothing about banking. She apologized for her ignorance, but he smiled and said, 'The ladies. The ladies. Never bother their pretty heads about such mundane things as money,' and then proceeded to give her a simple lecture on how to draw money as and when she needed it.

He then rang the bell and ordered tea and biscuits. Hannah asked a few questions and drank tea. Her voice began to sound strange and ugly in her ears. She had trained herself not to drop her aitches and to watch her grammar but now she felt it had a coarse sound compared to the cool and incisive voice of Sir George and the polite, cultured tones of the manager.

She was disappointed when the hundred pounds was handed to her in notes and silver. Hannah distrusted bank-notes, weak, flimsy pieces of paper. She preferred the hard, comfortable feel of gold.

When they left the bank and climbed in the coach, Sir George hesitated before giving instructions to his coachman to drive them back to Kensington. There was something

18

very rewarding about taking this odd housekeeper about. There was a wonderment in her eyes as she looked about the busy streets of London, something childlike. On a sudden impulse he raised the trap and said, 'Gunter's.'

Hannah flashed a look at him and then sat very still, the rigidity of her body hiding the bubbling excitement within. Gunter's was the famous pastry cook's and confectioner's in Berkeley Square. She wished that wretched and perfidious under-butler could see her now, Hannah Pym, entering the famous Gunter's on the arm of a gentleman, sitting down and eating cakes, like the veriest aristocrat.

'My brother must have been a sore trial to you in his latter years, Miss Pym,' said Sir George.

'Mr Clarence was never unkind or unreasonable, sir,' said Hannah. 'I felt for him. He had a broken heart. I do not know how Mrs Clarence, who was the soul of kindness, could have treated him so.'

'I do not think hearts break,' sighed Sir George. 'My brother was always moody and depressed even as a young man. Letitia Renfrew, as she was before she married him, was a great reader of Gothic novels. What she saw in my brother was brooding passion, very romantic. She was sadly mistaken. He must have been a sore trial to her.'

'Sir!' Hannah looked at him in amazement, her eyes suddenly as blue as her cloak. 'You surely do not condone such behaviour.'

He shrugged. 'I can understand it. My brother was set to become a recluse whether she stayed or went, in my opinion.'

'Do you know where Mrs Clarence is?' asked Hannah.

He shook his head.

'So pretty and kind,' mused Hannah. 'She is probably dead by now.'

'Why do you say that?'

'She was not brought up to work or even to scrimp and save. A footman's wages, even if he got another post, could not keep her, and besides, footmen are not allowed to marry or even to pretend to be married.'

'Letitia was a wealthy woman in her own right.'

'But surely that money would become her husband's when she married him?'

'No, she was protected by the marriage settlements. She would have enough to keep herself and her footman in comfort for life. Does that shock you?' he asked, looking at the housekeeper's startled face.

'I have been brought up to believe that the wicked are always punished,' said Hannah primly.

'Quite often not in this world. She was not wicked, only young and heedless, and tied to a man who must have made life seem like a desert.'

'But she has to live with her guilty conscience,' said Hannah.

'Perhaps. Have another cake. So where do you plan to travel first?'

'Exeter, sir.'

'Exeter! In midwinter with the snow falling? Why Exeter? Why not Brighton? That's a short run.'

'But it is the Exeter Fly that I watch going past,' said Hannah. 'I want to be on it. I want to see the house from the road.'

He took out his card case and extracted a card. 'I fear for you, Miss Pym,' he said. 'Take my card and come and see me on your return and let me know your adventures.'

'Oh, sir, I should be most honoured. How soon may I leave?'

'Let me see, Mr Entwhistle is coming in two days' time to Thornton Hall to pay off the few servants who qualify for the two hundred pounds. All the servants may as well be paid off at the same time. I will put a caretaker and his wife into Thornton Hall to keep it aired and cleaned until I decide to sell it. This can all be arranged quite quickly and there is really not much more for you to do. Say, in a week's time. Now what is troubling you?' he asked, seeing those odd eyes of hers lose colour.

Hannah gave a genteel cough. 'I have to confess, sir, that this cloak and hat are not my own. They belong to Mrs Clarence. She left all her clothes behind and. . . and. . . I could not . . . did not want to appear in servant's clothes on this momentous day. I wondered, sir, if I might pay you for them.'

'There is no need for that. Take what you wish, although no doubt everything is sadly outmoded. All your worries are over, Miss Pym. Relax and enjoy your cakes and look forward to your first journey on a Flying Machine.'

Hannah was by now Sir George's devoted slave. No one in all her life had treated her with such courtesy. He was a god. But some innate sensitivity made her mask her adoration. She feared that he might misread any admiration on her part and think this family servant was getting ideas above her station. She covertly looked around her at the well-bred faces, at the fearfully expensive clothes, at the snow whirling outside the leaded windows, at the piles of sweetmeats and pineapples and chocolate and fruit, and then at the high, arrogant face of Sir George Clarence and wondered if it were possible to die from sheer happiness. When they rose to leave, she shot quick little glances about her so that she might stamp the memory of this glorious afternoon on her mind for life.

To her disappointment, Sir George said he would not be staying at Thornton Hall. He would return in two days' time with the lawyer.

Hannah went up the stairs to Mrs Clarence's rooms that night when the other servants were asleep and took out coats and pelisses and mantles and hats and fine underwear like gossamer. Mrs Clarence had been slim as a young woman and of the same height as Hannah. Hannah did not want the other servants to know about Mrs Clarence's clothes. They were already bitterly jealous of her because of her large inheritance and the present of such fine clothes would only add to their jealousy.

*　　　*　　　*

The week passed like the stage-coach, rumbling off slowly and gathering momentum. Hannah tipped the Clarences' coachman to drive her into the City to purchase an inside ticket for the Exeter Fly. She then recklessly promised him more money if he would rise during the night to get her to the City to join the coach, which left at five in the morning. The coachman pointed out that she would need to pay for two grooms and the outside man as well as there was no way he was going to face the perils of Knightsbridge on his own. Hannah thought of her fortune and threw thrift to the winds. All that mattered now was to get on that coach.

There were so many preparations to make

in such a short time. But she had waited so long for an adventure, she could hardly bear to wait any longer. She took modest lodgings in Kensington Village and then packed as many of Mrs Clarence's clothes as she could into large trunks. The outside man wheeled them in a cart to her new home, two rooms above a bakery.

All that was left was the trunk to take on the journey.

She did not go to sleep the night before the Great Adventure, as she mentally called it. She walked about the house from room to room, seeing herself in every corner. There was the scullery maid Hannah bent over the pots, then kitchen maid Hannah over the stove, chambermaid Hannah screwing up her face as she took down the slops, then between-stairs maid Hannah polishing the oaken treads on the main staircase, then housemaid Hannah in the drawing-room, darting here and there, quick and light, and then her last shell, housekeeper Hannah, proud of her black gown and starched cap and with the bunch of keys jingling at her waist.

How happy she had been then! There was so much to do, so much pride in her new position. But after Mrs Clarence had run away and the staff of servants had shrunk and all the parties and callers and entertaining had ceased, time had hung heavy on her hands and her employer's depression seemed to permeate every room. And yet she was loyal to Mr Clarence and ever hopeful that one day Mrs Clarence might appear on the doorstep, gay and laughing, saying she had done it all for fun. But Mrs Clarence had never come back. At first Hannah had glanced idly out at the stage-coach going by. Bit by bit, she had begun to imagine herself on it, until she could not start her day until she had seen the coach thunder by. The sight of that coach made her feel less trapped in the gloom of Thornton Hall, where Mr Clarence grew more grey-faced and the servants moved silently about the house, as if in a house of mourning.

Sometimes she felt like yelling and singing, doing anything to shatter the grim silence, but respect for her employer was in her very bones. She had always been practical and busy until Mrs Clarence had run away, and then she gradually began to live in dreams of bowling along the dusty roads of England where the sun always shone, the birds always sang, and she was as free as the air. One Hannah saw that the rooms were aired and dusted and that the meals were served on time. The other Hannah, the inside Hannah, escaped far away outside the walls of Thornton Hall and into a dream country of endless travel and movement.

As the hour approached for the coachman to bring the carriage round, she began to worry and worry. What if the lazy old man was

25

still snoring? What if the grooms had refused to come?

But just when she had decided to walk over to the stables and find out, she heard the snorting of horses and the rumbling of wheels. She drew the blue cloak around her and settled the beaver hat more firmly on her head. A new century, a new life, a new Hannah.

She tugged open the main door and then turned briefly in salute, waving goodbye to her past, waving goodbye to her servant's life, as she had waved so many times to the Flying Machine on the Kensington Road.

Hannah slammed the door behind her with a satisfying final bang, handed up her trunk to the coachman, and climbed inside.

2

Before the Roman came to Rye or out to
  Severn strode,
The rolling English drunkard made the rolling
  English road.

G.K. Chesterton

Miss Hannah Pym would have found it hard to believe that members of the Quality regarded a journey by stage-coach as a sort of lingering death, preferring their own fast well-sprung carriages and teams of horses.

For to Hannah, standing, slightly open-mouthed, in the courtyard of the Bull and Gate in Aldersgate in the City of London at quarter to five on a freezing-cold morning, the stage-coach was romance on wheels. The coach was faced in dull black leather, thickly studded by way of ornament with broad black-headed nails tracing out the panels, in the upper part of which were four oval windows with heavy red wooden frames and leather curtains. Up on the roof, there were seats for the 'outsiders', surrounded by a high iron guard. In front of the outsiders sat the coachman and the guard, who always held his carbine ready cocked on his knees. Underneath them was a very long, narrow boot, or trunk, beneath a large spreading hammer-cloth hanging down on all sides and furnished with a luxuriant fringe. Behind the coach was the immense basket, stretching far and wide beyond the body, to which it was attached by long iron bars, or supports, passing underneath it. Travelling in the basket was cheap but highly uncomfortable.

A flake of snow drifted down and landed on Hannah's nose, then another. She climbed inside and, as she was the first, secured a seat by the window. The coachman, many-caped and red-faced, came lumbering and wheezing out and climbed up on the roof. Then came the other passengers. Hannah studied them

27

eagerly as they climbed in and took their places. There was a dainty woman in widow's weeds supported by a military-looking man who smelt strongly of brandy. They sat alongside Hannah. Opposite her was a beautiful young man, too fashionably dressed for coach travel. He saw Hannah looking at him in awe and hurriedly dropped his long lashes to veil a pair of violet eyes. Auburn hair glinted under a curly brimmed beaver and a slim boyish figure was wrapped in an immense cloak. Next to him was a very fat woman, and then, next to her, a dried-up stick of a man dressed in a black coat and breaches and sporting an old-fashioned Ramillies wig and a not-too-clean stock.

The City clocks began to chime five strokes. The guard on the roof blew a blast on his horn. And then a voice cried, 'Hold hard!' And the door beside Hannah was jerked open. Hannah noticed the youth opposite shrink back in his seat and pull his hat down over his eyes. The aristocratic-looking man who had jerked open the door had a hard, handsome saturnine face and black eyes. 'No room, hey?' he said. 'Better travel on top.' He slammed the door again. The coach dipped and swayed as he climbed on the roof. The guard blew a fanfare and the coach slowly lumbered forward.

The thin man in the black clothes was the first to break the silence. He passed cards all round and said he was a lawyer, name of Fletcher. 'If,' he said, 'in spite of highwaymen, snow-drifts, ruts a yard deep, we compass the one hundred and seventy-two miles, we may thank our stars when we land safe at the Swan at Exeter.' There was a murmur of agreement. The fat woman said she was Mrs Bradley, going home to Exeter after a visit to her married daughter. She fished in a capacious basket on her lap and produced a twist of paper which she said contained rhubarb pills, 'the only cure for sickness caused by the motion of the coach.' She said she hoped they would not go too fast, for she had a second cousin who had had an apoplexy brought on by the speed of a stage-coach. But, she went on, rummaging again in her basket, Dr Jameson's powders were the best thing for apoplexy, so if the rate of speed became too great, she urged the other passengers to avail themselves of this wonderful medicine.

The military man introduced himself as Captain Seaton. 'Never needed a pill or powder in me life,' he bragged. 'Little wife here knows that, don't you, Lizzie?' Lizzie blushed and murmured something inaudible. Hannah introduced herself briefly. The captain's eyes fastened on the young man. 'And what's your monicker, me young sprig?'

'Edward Smith,' said the young man and then closed his eyes firmly and pretended to go to sleep.

The rest all said they hoped to make the journey in the promised time of three days. Hannah studied them all avidly.

At Hyde Park toll, the guard jumped down to have a word with the toll-keeper, holding his carbine firmly. 'I hope he knows how to use that,' said the lawyer uneasily. 'I shall feel safer when we are through Knightsbridge.' For before the pretty village of Knightsbridge lay a place of bogs and highwaymen. Here the Great Western Road crossed a stream, the bed of which was composed of thick mud.

The guard climbed back up on the roof and the coach moved away from the line of whale-oil lamps at Hyde Park Corner and into the blackness that led to Knightsbridge. But all too soon, they reached the stream. Days earlier, Hannah had gone through this stream in Sir George's light carriage with barely a hitch. Even the Thornton Hall coach, which had deposited her in the City that morning, had stuck a little, but as it was lightly laden, had soon struggled clear.

But into this great impassable gulf of mud the Exeter Fly descended, and after desperate flounderings, stuck fast.

'Oh, dear, oh, dear,' said Mrs Bradley, clutching her precious basket. 'I hope there won't be no highwaymen. Reckon I'd die of fright, m'dears.'

Only Hannah remained calm. To her, the stagecoaches were impregnable fortresses on wheels. What villain would dare to accost the Exeter Fly?

'Stand and deliver!' shouted a great voice from outside. The fat woman screamed, the captain turned a muddy colour, his wife buried her face in her hands, the lawyer swore quite dreadfully, and the slim youth, Edward Smith, sat up with a start and looked around, wild-eyed. 'Are they come for me?' he asked Hannah.

Before Hannah could ask him what he meant, the voice shouted again. 'Outside, all of you in there.'

They climbed out, Hannah conscious the whole time of the money in her reticule. They were all standing now with freezing muddy water half-way up their legs. The highwayman had dismounted and was brandishing a brace of pistols. 'Bad pickings,' he commented sourly on seeing the inside passengers. 'Poor lot. Turn out your—'

That was as far as he got. He was struck a vicious blow from behind and collapsed into the muddy water. Looming over him appeared the aristocrat of the roof, the hard-faced saturnine man. He dragged the highwayman clear of the mud and water and laid him on the road and bound his hands behind his back. 'Thank you, sir,' said Hannah. 'I am most grateful to you.'

'Of course,' blustered Captain Seaton, 'I was just about to take action meself, but my lady wife had come over faint, don't you see, and I could hardly leave her.'

The aristocrat of the roof did not reply. The guard was unfastening one of the leaders so as to ride to the Half-Way public house between Kensington and Knightsbridge to get help. He roused the watch on the way, and two watchmen came to march the now conscious highwayman off to the nearest roundhouse. The guard returned with a squad of men. All the passengers, who had climbed back into the coach for shelter, were ordered to dismount. The leader was hitched up again, and with a great shoving and pulling, the Exeter Fly was back on the road.

It was only then that the inside passengers realized the full discomfort of wet and frozen feet. 'We cannot proceed,' said Hannah firmly to the coachman. 'We are all soaked and like to catch the ague.'

'Get as far as the Half-Way house,' said the aristocrat, 'and get the ladies a room where they may change into dry clothes.'

'And just who's giving the orders around here?' demanded the coachman with heavy sarcasm.

'The man who is about to buy every man jack of you as much rum and hot water as you can drink,' he replied coolly.

'Now, that's different,' said the coachman. 'Very.'

At the Half-Way public house, Mrs Seaton,

Mrs Bradley and Hannah had their trunks borne upstairs to a bleak room above the pub and began to look out dry clothes. Hannah thanked God she had had the foresight to put another of Mrs Clarence's cloaks in her capacious trunk. The cloak was of red merino lined with fur. She changed into one of her own black wool gowns and a flannel petticoat, also of her own, wool stockings and half-boots, crammed her beaver on her head, and turned her attention to her two companions. Mrs Seaton had taken more black items of clothing out of a trunk that seemed to contain nothing but black clothes. She was probably much older than she appeared, thought Hannah. In her thirties, perhaps late thirties. Mrs Bradley's trunk seemed to contain a great deal of foodstuff: a trussed chicken, two jars of jam, a ham, and a large jar of pickles. But somewhere at the bottom she found fresh clothes, or rather a change of clothes, for the smell that arose from her new wardrobe was a powerful mixture of sweat and moth-balls and benzine.

When they descended to the taproom, it was to find a merry party going on. Edward Smith and Captain Seaton had both been wearing top-boots and had not had to change, but the lawyer, who had been wearing buckled shoes and stockings and who could not be bothered changing his clothes, was sitting huddled by the fire with his shoes stuffed with newspaper on the hearth and his wet stockings hanging over the high fender.

A glass of rum and hot water was handed to Hannah. She looked at it doubtfully. In this hard-drinking age, servants drank as much as their betters, but not Hannah. But she was still cold and she did not want to fall ill and therefore never be able to have any more adventures. For Hannah, now that the peril of the highwayman was over, felt elated and happy and ready to tackle any frights the journey had to offer. Still, she hesitated. She had never drunk anything stronger than coffee in her life. She had seen too many female servants end up in trouble through a fondness for strong drink. She squinted down her nose at the rum and sniffed it cautiously. She became aware of being watched and looked up. The tall aristocrat was leaning against the corner of the high mantelpiece, scrutinizing her with a look of amusement in his black eyes. 'Your health, madam,' he said, raising his own glass.

'Your health, sir,' echoed Hannah and, screwing up her eyes, she downed the contents of the glass in one go. She gasped and choked and Mrs Bradley slapped her on the back. The rum then settled in Hannah's stomach and a warm glow began to spread through her thin body. The aristocrat had turned away to speak to the landlord. She studied him curiously. Perhaps he was not an aristocrat, but merely some adventurer. But then, he had an air of command, of authority, and his blue coat was expensively cut and of the finest material. Underneath it, he wore a striped waistcoat over a ruffled shirt. A sign of aristocratic arrogance, or sheer bravery, was that he wore the shirt ruffles at his wrists in full display. Since the French Revolution, still called the Bourgeois Revolution, and the American War of Independence, still called the Colonial Wars, gentlemen were careful not to flaunt their rank before the common people. Strangely enough, what could drive a London mob roaming the streets looking for trouble into violence was the sight of a gentleman sporting ruffles or a band of white at the wrists, that little display of linen which drew the line between gentleman and commoner. This gentleman was wearing, instead of one of the cocked hats that were only just going out of fashion, a wide-brimmed hat with a low crown.

Hannah turned her attention to Mrs Seaton, sitting by the fire with her captain. Very odd, thought Hannah, her eyes darting with curiosity. Everything black. Of course her father or mother could just have died, rather than a former husband, and she might have married the captain before the period of mourning was up. What an odd sort of husband the captain was—too loud and beefy and gross for such a dainty woman.

35

Then the coachman was shrugging on his greatcoat and wrapping a massive woollen shawl about his shoulders and calling to the passengers to take their places. Mr Fletcher, the lawyer, unhitched his stockings from the fender and put them on, modestly turning his back on the company as he pulled them on over white stick-like legs criss-crossed with purple varicose veins. Hannah found herself getting quite excited at the sight, not because she found the poor lawyer's legs attractive, but because the conventions were being shed, one by one, at an early part of the Great Adventure. They were all explorers, she thought, giving a genteel hiccup, heading out into the jungle of the unknown.

Fresh straw had been put in the carriage and, luxury of luxuries, hot bricks. 'Probably that there gran' gennelman, m'dears,' said Mrs Bradley. 'Coachman would never get landlord to busy hisself with our comfort.'

'Grand gentleman, pooh!' said Captain Seaton. 'Something wrong with that fellow, if you ask me. Adventurer, mountebank or deserter. Yes, yes. Just mark my words.'

Off they went. The coach began to pick up speed as it moved through Kensington Village. And then they were racing along the long straight road that led past Thornton Hall. Deaf to cries of outrage from the other passengers, Hannah seized the leather strap and let down the glass and hung out of the window. There was the square box of Thornton Hall. No smoke was rising from the chimneys. With me gone, thought Hannah, the lazy dogs are probably all still abed. 'Goodbye!' she shouted, and then pulled up the glass and sat down, smiling into the glaring eyes of the other passengers.

'How come you did that there?' demanded Mrs Bradley. 'You're like to kill us all with cold.'

'I am sorry,' said Hannah. 'I was saying goodbye.'

'To what?' asked Edward Smith suddenly.

'To my past,' said Hannah grandly, and then smiled in what she hoped was an enigmatic way.

The snow began to fall, not very heavily, but in large, pretty flakes. The coach moved slowly on through the winter landscape. Hannah's head began to nod. Although she never slept very much, she had had no sleep at all the night before. She had a very odd dream. She was back at a servants' dance in the servants' hall and waiting for the arrival of Mr and Mrs Clarence to grace the festivities. When they came in, he looked, as usual, a brooding, handsome man, but Mrs Clarence was dressed as a Shakespearian page in doublet and hose and with a little cloak hanging from one shoulder. 'Disgraceful,' Mr Clarence began to shout. 'How dare you dress as a boy!'

37

The coach jolted over a rut and Hannah awoke with a start. What a strange dream. It had been so vivid. And yet Mrs Clarence had never dressed as a boy. Hannah's eyes fell on Edward Smith, now asleep opposite. Surely that was the reason for her dream, for Edward was pretty enough to be a girl masquerading as a boy.

Hannah's head began to nod again.

The coach stopped at the Pigeons at Brentford, and the passengers alighted to take breakfast. A silly argument broke out between the coachman and the captain. The captain said Brentford was a fine town and the coachman said it was a filthy place. The captain said it was noted for the best post-horses. 'Ho, is that so?' sneered the coachman. 'Well, let me tell you, sir, there war two posting-horses here what got so tired of the vile paving-stones what adorns this here town that they tried for to commit suicide by drowning themselves in the Grand Canal. And would ha' done it, too, pore things, had not a clergyman come along and told them it was wicked and that the horses' hell was paved wi' broken glass.' The captain, who should have known that very few could out-talk a coachman, fell into a brooding silence.

The snow was falling thicker now. The talk among the passengers, however, was not of the snow but of the perils of Hounslow Heath, which lay in front of them. The captain, full of

Nantes brandy and bluster, said he would down any highwaymen who tried to stop them and cursed Hannah under his breath when she said sharply that he had not been too ready to down the last one. Hannah had taken a dislike to the captain.

At the town of Hounslow, they were advised by the landlord of the George not to go forward, as the Bath Flying Machine up to town had been snowed up beyond Colnbrook, and that he had beds aired and ready for them. The coachman, full of valour, called for more brandy and joined the captain in the bar.

Inspired by a large quantity of brandy, the coachman now thought himself to be Jehu, son of Nimshi, and the Fly left Hounslow behind it at a good round six miles an hour.

The first thing to be seen on the notorious Hounslow Heath was the Salisbury coach in a terrific snow-drift; or rather, the coachman's hat, two horses' heads, the roof of the coach, and two passengers standing on their luggage, bawling, 'Help!' The coachman of the Exeter Fly seemed to regard this disaster as a mere landmark and drove on.

The snow was falling thicker and faster. The horses went slower and slower. The coachman tried fanning them, towelling them and chopping them—which, translated, meant hitting them hard, harder, and hardest. The six horses slowed to a walk and could only be made to go ahead by oaths and curses. The

39

coach took nearly three hours to cover the seven miles from Hounslow to the Bush at Staines. In the language of the day, the passengers all gave themselves up for gone. But as they drew up outside the Bush at Staines, the sun broke through the clouds and the snow ceased to fall.

The landlord counselled rest and dinner, and the passengers, who had never before in their lives come so near to the experience of travelling in a hollowed-out iceberg, were inclined to take his advice. But success, stimulant and a lull in the snowstorm had made the coachman daring. 'I be an Englishman,' he growled, 'and I be inning at Bagshot this here night, and any yellow-bellies can stay behind.' Hannah looked to the aristocrat for support, but he was standing over by the window, detached from the group.

The party left the inn for the courtyard and voted on whether to go or stay. They stood outside the coach, beating their arms and stamping their feet as they made their votes. Only Hannah slipped away to arrange rescue for the Salisbury coach, the landlord of the Bush saying he would set out with his men himself, delighted at the possibility of guests now that it seemed as if the Exeter Fly meant to go on.

Emboldened by yet more brandy, the captain took the opportunity to show off to his wife and the party by saying, b'Gad, he, too,

40

was an Englishman and would face any peril that the journey could offer. The others were reluctant to be left behind, and so the passengers boarded the coach again, and, to faint hurrahs from the half-frozen post-boys, they set out on the road. At Egham, one mile and three furlongs on, it began to snow again.

The coachman pulled up at the Catherine Wheel for another glass of fortifier and then the coach set out once more.

Now the snow was falling as it should fall at Christmastime, when men are snug in parlours in front of blazing fires and not out braving the blasts in a Flying Machine. The coachman, foreseeing the worst, since at every moment the snowfall was becoming heavier, tried to churn his horses into a canter as the gloom of a winter's afternoon settled on Bagshot Heath. The guard beside him fingered his carbine delicately and stared anxiously about for highwaymen, but the coachman said no highwayman would be stupid enough to be out of doors in such weather. The guard said that it was due to the coachman's stupidity that they were all out of doors themselves, to which the coachman replied that the guard always had been a milksop, to which the guard, mad with passion, screamed at the coachman: 'I 'ates you like pison!' and fired his carbine in the air.

Captain Seaton, the effects of the brandy he had drunk beginning to fade, had been seeing a highwayman behind every bush.

At the sound of the shot from the roof, he wrenched open the door of the coach and jumped into a snow-drift. At the same time, the coachman drove into a rut a yard deep and the coach stuck fast.

The coachman doubled-thonged his wheelers, who dragged the coach out to the side of the road. . . and the whole coach slowly overturned into a gravel pit.

Chaos reigned inside the coach. Everyone was lying on top of everyone else in a jumble of arms and legs. The door above them opened, showing them the coachman's ruddy face and the sky behind him. 'Better come out o' there,' he said and disappeared.

He was replaced by the aristocrat, who lifted Hannah out, then Mrs Seaton, the youth, the lawyer, and then finally, with a great heaving, Mrs Bradley.

'You are a Trojan, sir,' said Hannah to their rescuer. 'I am Miss Hannah Pym.'

He smiled and swept off his hat. 'And I, Miss Pym, am Harley. Lord Ranger Harley.'

Behind Miss Pym, the youth gave a slight moan and fainted dead away.

'Puny little fellow,' said Lord Harley with contempt. 'Move aside, Miss Pym, and I will rub some snow on his face.'

In a flash, Hannah remembered her dream about Mrs Clarence. Something made her say urgently, 'No, leave him to me.'

42

Lord Harley strode off and cut the traces and led one of the wheelers free, mounted it and rode off in search of help. All the other horses were, amazingly, unharmed.

While Hannah knelt down beside the fallen youth, the other passengers and the coachman and guard stood around in half-frozen attitudes, including Captain Seaton, who was cursing and mumbling and swearing blind he had seen a highwayman.

Hannah loosened Edward's clothing and discovered that her budding suspicions had been right. 'Edward' was in fact not a beautiful young man but a beautiful young woman. But something prompted Hannah to help this girl keep up her disguise. She held a bottle of smelling-salts under the girl's nose and watched those violet eyes flutter open. Then the eyes became wider with fear. 'Hush,' said Hannah, 'do not say anything. Help is on the way.' She raised the girl to her feet and kept close beside her.

The coachman was now sitting on a mound of snow drinking brandy, occasionally putting his flask down and moving his arms as if driving phantom horses. The guard had replaced his carbine with a blunderbuss. A sudden movement in the snow made him shout, 'Highwayman!', and point his blunderbuss. And the curious shepherd who had approached from behind a bush to view the stranded party turned too late to flee and got his backside peppered with shot. Hannah was reluctant to leave the girl, but something had to be done for the poor man. Mrs Bradley, revived from her dismal frozen torpor by the sight of the accident, bustled after Hannah carrying her basket and rummaging in it for all sorts of medicines to relieve pain. The shepherd was given brandy by the guard and then the ladies placed the afflicted man next to the coachman.

Hannah returned to the girl's side. She was standing huddled beside the overturned coach in the shelter of the shallow pit. 'Do not worry,' said Hannah, 'Lord Harley will fetch help.' The girl shuddered and turned her face away.

Just when Hannah began to think she would never be able to feel her feet or hands again, she saw lights bobbing across the snow. The rescue party had arrived and kept on coming despite the fact that the guard shouted, 'Foot-pads!' and fired in its direction.

There was no sign of Lord Harley, but there was the landlord of the Nag's Head at Bagshot, who had been told of the travellers' plight by Lord Harley, beaming all over his face at the thought of visitors, and leading stable-boys carrying torches and ostlers carrying staves. There was also plenty of brandy for the frost-bitten and a post-chaise for the wounded.

The coach was righted and the horses

hitched to it again. The captain commandeered the post-chaise for himself and his wife and the shepherd travelled inside with the lawyer, consulting him about damages.

Freezing and weary, the travellers entered the inn at Bagshot to find themselves facing the best welcome an English inn could offer the storm-bound stagecoach traveller. A great fire blazed, and on a huge long table sat iris-tinted rounds of beef, marble-veined ribs, gelatinous veal pies, colossal hams, gallons of old ale, bottles of wine, raised pies, tartlets, fruit and jellies and custard.

Hannah was never to forget that welcome. No one wanted to change out of his wet clothes; they were all too tired and hungry. Hannah could not ever remember being quite so ravenous. They all sat around the table. Lord Harley was already there. Having sent out help, he said he had seen no need to go along with it. There were the two other outside passengers: a round-faced farmer and a shabby gentleman with a pleasant face. The farmer said his name was Mr Burridge, and the shabby gentleman introduced himself as Mr Hendry.

They made a jolly party, Mrs Bradley telling all and sundry that she had a little jar of goose fat, the best thing for chilblains.

But as they ate themselves stiff and drank themselves silly, a certain acrimony began to

45

creep in. The guard, still smarting from the coachman's insult, started to mutter about the folly of being tied to a drunken sot.

The captain began to feel his nose had been put out of joint by this Lord Harley and began to talk darkly about adventurers and penniless younger sons who were no better than they should be. His wife tried to hush him; he snarled at her, and she looked at him in horrified amazement. The captain rallied and patted her hand and said he was the worst of beasts.

Lord Harley was studying 'Edward', and Hannah did not like the growing gleam of amusement in those dark eyes. He started to raise his glass to Edward, saying, 'Take wine with me, Mr Smith.' The custom demanded that Edward drink a glass of wine and raise a glass in return.

The landlord came in to say that the bedchambers were all ready and it was time to decide who slept in the same bedchamber with whom, 'And be sure the party is congenial,' he joked, 'for you've got to share the same bed.'

The first surprise was when Mrs Seaton said in a trembling voice, 'I shall share with Mrs Bradley.'

'Come now, my dove,' said the captain, affecting a hearty laugh. 'You have had too much to drink.'

'I have not had too much to drink,' said Lizzie in a wobbly voice. 'I am not Mrs

Seaton, I am Mrs Lizzie Bisley, widow, and we are not yet wed, Captain Seaton, and I will not share your bed until we are.'

There was a stunned silence.

'We're as good as married,' said the captain, breaking the silence. 'We're to be married in Exeter.'

Good heavens, thought Hannah, her nose twitching with excitement. Lizzie is not Mrs Seaton, and Edward is not Edward. Whatever next?

'O' course you can share with me, my duck,' said Mrs Bradley, her eyes flashing. 'Fie, for shame, Cap'n. You pigs o' men can't wait to get your leg o'er a lass. Come along, come along. I'll make you a posset and you'll sleep like a log.'

The captain stared ferociously into his glass while Mrs Bradley led Lizzie away. 'That's a fine woman, a fine woman, Seaton,' said the little lawyer, Mr Fletcher, with unexpected ferocity, 'and deserving of every courtesy and kindness.'

'Want to make something of it?' sneered the captain.

'Yes,' said Mr Fletcher, jumping to his feet, his wig askew. He bunched his thin fingers into fists and panted, 'I'll draw your cork.'

'Sit down,' ordered Lord Harley. 'No one is going to fight anyone. Have we not all endured enough? Back to the sleeping arrangements, if you please.' His eyes glinted

47

oddly at Edward. 'I suggest Mr Smith and I will get along tolerably well.'

Edward turned milk-white. Hannah rose to her feet and leaned on the table and glared at Lord Harley. 'That will not answer, my lord, and well you know it.'

'Indeed, Miss Pym,' said his lordship in a silky voice. 'And may I ask why?'

'I am not Edward Smith,' said the girl in a voice that shook pathetically. 'I am Miss Emily Freemantle.'

'I thought so,' said Lord Harley laconically. 'You don't make a very convincing man.'

'Hey!' said the landlord. 'What's a goin' on?'

'My family betrothed me to that monster against my wishes,' said Emily. 'I ran away. I am going to my old nurse at Exeter until they change their minds and call off this disgusting marriage.'

'I do not want to marry a silly little chit like you,' said Lord Harley icily.

'Then why did you come after me?' demanded Emily. She had made an odd figure, dining with her beaver hat on. She took it off and placed it on a chair beside her, revealing a crop of auburn curls.

'Your parents, minx, guessed where you had gone and I volunteered to search the posting-inns for you,' said Lord Harley. 'Did you never stop for one moment to think of the distress you were causing them?'

'Why?' said Emily in a voice thick with tears. 'They never thought of me. They know I am in love with Mr Peregrine Williams, but did they listen? No! "You are to marry Lord Ranger Harley," they said. You are old, sir, and have the reputation of the devil.'

'Why did you both not recognize each other?' asked Hannah.

'Because we had never met,' said Emily. 'My family want his money and title. They are not interested in finding out if we might care for each other.'

'Put your mind at rest, child,' said Lord Harley in a bored voice, 'and stop enacting Haymarket tragedies before the interested public of this inn. I was given to understand you wished the marriage. Now I have seen you, I do not wish to be married to you any more than you wish to be married to me. You will return to London with me and marry this Mr Williams if you wish.'

There was a long silence again.

The landlord cleared his throat. 'What a coil,' he said. 'Is there anyone else here who isn't a miss or a man or who ain't married or who's running away? Or can I get you all off to bed?'

'You shall come with me,' said Hannah firmly to Emily.

Overwrought, Emily burst into tears. Hannah helped her to her feet and led her from the room. 'Blue Room,' shouted the landlord. 'Top o' the stairs and turn right.'

Hannah Pym thought she would die from curiosity. So many complications! But, like bad knitting, surely all that was needed was for them to be unravelled by an expert and made up again in the right way.

3

I have heard with admiring submission the experience of the lady who declared that the sense of being well-dressed gives a feeling of inward tranquillity which religion is powerless to bestow.

Ralph Waldo Emerson

The Blue Room was comfortable and well appointed, with low rafters, chintz curtains at the window, and cheerful chintz hangings on the bed. A fire burnt brightly in the small hearth. There were two easy chairs in front of the fire, and it was into one of these chairs that Hannah thrust Emily. She then took off her cloak and hung it on a peg behind the door, along with her hat, before sitting down opposite the girl.

'Now, what is all this about?' said Hannah, trying to keep her vulgar gossipy eagerness in check. The girl was so very beautiful with those large violet eyes and auburn hair. Her face was a well-shaped oval with a small straight nose.

'I think I should know to whom I am talking,' said Emily with a pathetic attempt at hauteur.

'I am Miss Hannah Pym, gentlewoman of Kensington,' said Hannah firmly. Her servant days were behind her now, and she was determined not to stifle any confidences by revealing she had lately been in service.

'And do you have relatives in Exeter, Miss Pym?'

'No, I am simply travelling for the sake of travel.'

Despite her distress, Emily gave a reluctant laugh. What an odd lady this Miss Pym was with her strange eyes and crooked nose. 'I cannot possibly imagine anyone travelling on the stage for *fun*,' she said.

'But I have already had a great many adventures,' said Hannah, her eyes glowing gold in the firelight. 'Just think. A real highwayman. A widow who is not the captain's wife. And now you, not a boy but a pretty lady running away from a man who does not seem to want her after all.'

'I do not believe him,' said Emily. 'It is a trick.'

'Who is this Lord Harley?'

'Lord Ranger Harley,' said Emily in a clear voice, 'is a rake and a libertine.'

'How so?'

'I happen to know, for my governess told me, that he has an opera dancer in keeping.'

'Do you still have a governess?' asked Miss Pym, momentarily diverted. 'I would have thought you too old.'

'I am eighteen,' said Emily haughtily. 'But Miss Cudlipp, that is my governess's name, is dear to me. She stays as a sort of companion. She is very wise.'

Hannah sniffed. She thought that Miss Cudlipp was downright disloyal to her employers to pour scandal about Emily's intended into the girl's ears. 'But this business about the opera dancer,' said Hannah. 'That is merely gossip. She cannot know for sure.'

'Miss Cudlipp knows everything,' said Emily. 'Oh, what am I to do? He will force me to go back with him and marry him.'

'Really, Miss Freemantle, if you will forgive me, he did not look at all the sort of man who would have to force any woman to marry him. He is very handsome and he is a lord. Is he rich?'

'Very,' said Emily in a hollow voice.

'Then there you are. He cannot possibly want to marry you.'

'He does not like to be thwarted. Miss Cudlipp said so.'

Hannah mentally sent Miss Cudlipp and all her sayings to the devil. 'So who is Mr Peregrine Williams?'

Emily turned a delicate shade of pink. 'He

52

is charming, so very fair and beautiful. He has hair like gold and the bluest eyes you have ever seen. He writes poetry to me which Miss Cudlipp says rivals Mr Wordsworth.'

'And did your parents introduce you to this paragon?'

'Oh, no. It transpires that they had set their hearts on my marrying Harley a long time ago. I have not even made my come-out. I met Mr Williams when I was walking in the Park with Miss Cudlipp. I would not have noticed him, but Miss Cudlipp said, "Regard that beautiful young man who watches you so closely." I looked across and he was standing under a tree, a book in his hand. He looked at me so intently, I began to tremble. But Miss Cudlipp with great bravery approached him and asked him why he was staring, and he said. . . do you know what he said?'

' " "Your beauty has pierced my heart," or some such thing?' suggested Hannah.

'Well. . . not exactly, but he said, "The fair maiden yonder has struck my heart a blow. I am blinded by her beauty." '

'Fiddlesticks,' muttered Miss Pym.

'What did you say?'

'I said "Fiddlesticks" because I thought the fire was dying down,' said Hannah. 'Go on about Mr Williams.'

'He begged permission to call, and so I gave him my direction,' said Emily. 'But when he called, my parents refused to have him

53

admitted. They then asked around the town about him and found that although of gentle birth, he has little money, and so I received a terrible punishment.'

'They beat you?'

'No, they took my novels.'

Very proper, thought Hannah. Aloud she said, 'So you never saw him again?'

'Of course I did! Miss Cudlipp saw to that.'

'Yes, of course she would,' said Hannah. 'But, believe me, as we are going to be trapped in this hostelry for a few days, I would suggest you make a friend of this Lord Harley. You will find that not only does he not want to marry you, but that he might break that sad news very tactfully to your parents.'

Emily's beautiful face took on a mulish look. 'He will not change his mind.'

'Why?'

'Because I am very beautiful.'

Hannah was thoroughly shocked. 'You must not say such a thing, my dear Miss Freemantle.'

'Why not?'

'Because anyone who praises her own looks immediately appears vain and shabby.'

'Miss Cudlipp says—'

'Never mind what Miss Cudlipp says. Did that governess encourage you to flee?'

'Oh, yes. 'Twas most exciting. I climbed down from my bedroom window and she lowered the trunks down to me.'

'And where did you get the men's clothes?'

'They are my brother's. He is at sea. He is much older than I—twenty-five—and these are the clothes he wore when he was my age. He had not thrown them away.'

Emily yawned. 'You had best get to bed,' said Hannah, her mind racing. 'You do have women's clothes with you?'

'Yes, in my trunk. I only have this one suit of men's clothes and two clean shirts and neckcloths and two pairs of small-clothes and unmentionables.'

The door opened and two waiters came in bearing their trunks. Emily had two enormous trunks that made Hannah's one serviceable trunk look modest.

Hannah tipped the waiters and then threw open the lid of her trunk and took out the clothes that had become soiled in the stream in Knightsbridge. 'I will just take these down to the kitchen and see if anyone knows how to clean and press them,' said Hannah.

Emily rose and yawned and staggered slightly. 'I feel quite drunk,' she said with a giggle.

Hannah picked up her soiled clothes and went down to the kitchen. Mrs Silvers, the landlord's wife, was giving instructions to the cook. She took the clothes from Hannah and said she would see that the linen was washed and that the mud was brushed from the other items when they were dry, for they were all

55

still damp from their soaking. Hannah then regaled the landlord's wife with a vivid account of her adventures. Mrs Silvers listened open-mouthed and then ran to fetch her husband, and Hannah had to tell her story all over again. The landlord was greatly intrigued and said she told a rare tale. Producing a bottle of French brandy, he poured Hannah a measure. Hannah was beginning to feel like a sot. After a lifetime of abstinence, she seemed to be making up for it all in a short space of time.

But the brandy, instead of making her feel sleepy, seemed to activate her busy brain more.

She returned to the Blue Room. Emily was in bed and asleep, looking young and defenceless. Her discarded clothes were scattered all over the room.

Not a bad child, thought Hannah, but thoroughly spoilt. How amazing the amount of damage that can be done by one silly governess. She moved about picking up the clothes. Emily's trunks were open. On the top of one was a man's shirt and clean neckcloth. Hannah picked the shirt up and took it over to the fire, where a lamp was still burning on a side-table. It was ruffled and of the finest cambric. She returned to the trunk and without a shred of conscience searched its contents. She was relieved to find that Emily had spoken the truth. There were only a few items of men's clothing. The rest was an assortment of beautiful gowns and underwear. Apart from Emily's two trunks, there was a large hat box, lying open, hats spilling over the floor. Hannah clucked in irritation and carried them over to the wardrobe and put them on the capacious upper shelf. Among the hats was the man's wig. No doubt Emily had meant to use it as part of her disguise and had cut her hair short instead. Hannah carried it to a wig-stand and then studied it. It was a fine wig of real hair, white and curled and tied at the back with a black silk ribbon.

She returned to Emily's trunks and took out dresses and pelisses and mantles and hung them away and then arranged the underwear in the top half of the chest of drawers. Then she opened her own modest trunk and put her own things away. She carried her hairbrush and pin-box to the toilet table. It was already crammed with silver-topped bottles of lotions and creams, brushes, combs and bone pins, Emily having unpacked her toilet things. The towels were damp and had been thrown on the floor, and it appeared Emily had used up both cans of hot water.

Hannah rang the bell and gave the chambermaid the empty cans and basin of dirty water and the soiled towels and asked for a replacement.

She kept on working until everything was put away and the trunks and bandbox stowed

57

under the bed. The maid returned with fresh towels and hot water. Hannah knew that such luxuries would be put on the bill and was determined Emily should pay for them.

Her gaze fell on that wig, gleaming whitely on the wig-stand. She picked it up, then a clean neckcloth, and then the cambric shirt, and made her way downstairs and asked where she might find the lawyer, Mr Fletcher. She was told he was sharing the Red Room— 'Top of the stairs and turn left'—with Lord Harley.

Hannah went up to the Red Room and, forgetting that she was no longer a servant but a guest at the inn, failed to knock, but simply turned the handle and opened the door.

There was a squawk of dismay from Mr Fletcher. The lawyer was stark naked, sitting in a hip-bath in front of the fire. Lord Harley was scrubbing his back.

Hannah retreated.

She waited outside the door, and after a few moments Lord Harley came out and closed the door behind him. 'What is it, Miss Pym? And do you never knock?'

The answer to that was, 'No, good servants never knock,' but Hannah had no intention of letting Lord Harley or anyone else know she had been a servant.

'I am sorry, my lord,' said Hannah. 'I am sleepy and forgot.'

He thought she looked remarkably wide

58

awake, and was further amazed that the sight of a naked man had not even raised a blush to this spinster's cheek. He could not know that Hannah was accustomed, from her days in the lower ranks of servants, to coming across gentlemen in the buff.

Hannah held out the wig, shirt, and neckcloth. 'Miss Freemantle will not be needing these items, and I thought Mr Fletcher might appreciate a fresh change of shirt and perhaps a new wig. Mr Fletcher is thin and Miss Freemantle is slim and I felt sure the shirt would fit.'

Lord Harley's lips curled in amusement. Poor Mr Fletcher. There had been no doubt that Mr Fletcher was slightly ripe. Lord Harley had cajoled him into taking a bath, not wanting to share the bed with a smelly stranger. 'You had best give these things to me,' he said, opening the door again to enter. 'Tact is called for. Wait there.'

'I have come upon some fresh articles of clothing,' said Lord Harley, putting shirt, wig and neckcloth on a chair beside the bath. 'Pray give me your soiled linen and I will take it to the kitchen for washing.'

'Very well,' said Mr Fletcher, trying to cover himself modestly with a large bar of soap. 'But these things were washed last month.'

'Another washing won't harm them,' said Lord Harley. 'Do you have fresh linen?'

'In my trunk,' said Mr Fletcher, feeling like

59

a schoolboy.

Lord Harley searched in it and found items which he noticed were actually fresh and clean. He scooped up Mr Fletcher's discarded underwear and shirt. 'Do not wait up for me,' he ordered. 'Leave the bath and I shall send a couple of waiters up to take it away.'

Mr Fletcher nodded dumbly. He was not insulted. He thought this bathing thing was a mad foible of the aristocracy, but he was too overwhelmed at the honour of being looked after by a real-live lord to protest.

Lord Harley went out and joined Hannah on the landing. 'I will take these from you,' said Hannah briskly.

'No, I shall come with you. It is early yet.'

He followed Hannah to the kitchen and watched as she gave orders for the clothes to be washed and pointed to a couple of minute tears and asked that they might be stitched.

'Put it on my bill,' said Lord Harley to the landlord, who was sitting at the kitchen table eating a late supper. Hannah stifled a sigh of relief. She was thrifty by nature and her recent elevation to the ranks of the middle class had made her realize that five thousand pounds had to be guarded carefully. 'Is there anyone in the coffee room?' Lord Harley asked.

'No, your honour,' said the landlord, Mr Silvers. 'They's all abed.'

'Then have a bottle of brandy sent up. Miss Pym and I have much to discuss.'

Hannah's eyes flashed green with excitement. But although she was happy to let the thought of drinking brandy with a lord go to her head, she was worried about the effects of so much alcohol, and when they were seated in the coffee room before the fire, she asked for only a little to be poured for her.

The wind howled ferociously outside, and snow whispered busily against the glass of the bay window that overlooked the courtyard of the inn.

'Nasty weather,' said Lord Harley. 'I fear it will be a few days before any of us can move.'

'Yes, indeed,' said Hannah happily. She felt she had walked out of the wings on to the centre stage for the first time in her life. There was so very much to interest her in the other guests.

'Now to Miss Freemantle,' said Lord Harley, stretching out his booted legs to the fire. They were very handsome legs, Hannah noticed. Hannah firmly believed that any gentleman with good legs was set for life. No one bothered about his face so long as he had good legs.

'Has she spoken to you of this sad affair?' he asked.

'Yes,' said Hannah. 'It appears her head was filled by a lot of rubbish about you by her governess, a Miss Cudlipp. This Miss Cudlipp told Miss Freemantle you had an opera dancer in keeping.'

61

'The deuce she did! And does that make me a monster?'

'To an impressionable young girl who has not yet made her come-out and has had no influence on her mind other than that given it by novels and by one addle-pated governess— yes.'

'What a coil,' he mused. 'I had planned to marry, to settle down, you know how it is. My aunt sent me a miniature of the Freemantle chit with a long story about how the girl had seen me in the Park and had fallen instantly in love. Miss Freemantle is from a good background. I thought it time to marry. My affections were not engaged. Mr and Mrs Freemantle came to see me. My lawyers met their lawyers. All was arranged. I thought it time to call and see this maiden who was so enamoured of me. The house was in an uproar. Maiden fled. Aunt had lied. Governess interrogated. Yes, she is a vastly silly woman. At last, parents decide the girl has gone to Exeter to visit her old nurse. I thought that if I took the stage myself and asked at inns and posting-houses on the road, I might catch up with her. Why on earth does she think I might want to marry her now?'

'Because she is so very beautiful.'

'Did she say that?'

'I think it was more the voice of Miss Cudlipp speaking in her head.'

'Talk some sense into her, Miss Pym, I beg

62

of you. She might do something silly, like running off into the snow.'

'I shall do my best,' said Hannah, 'but the damage done by a silly governess is hard to counteract in a short space of time.'

'What takes you to Exeter, Miss Pym?'

'I have never seen Exeter.'

'I do not understand.'

'I have a wish to travel,' said Hannah, clasping her long, thin fingers.'

'On the common stage?'

'The stage-coaches are not common to me,' said Hannah. 'I used to watch them going along the Kensington Road. All that motion and adventure.'

'You live in Kensington?'

'Yes, at Thornton Hall.'

Lord Harley looked at her curiously. 'You must be one of the Clarences.'

'Distantly related, my lord,' said Hannah, quickly lowering her eyes.

'Indeed? And which branch of the family would that be?'

Hannah felt a stab of panic. The aristocracy and gentry knew everything about everyone. It was their way of making sure that no interloper or adventurer broke into their gilded ranks. There were ladies, Hannah knew, who did little else but discuss families and relations.

She looked miserably into her brandy glass and prayed for inspiration.

'You are not running away as well?' asked Lord Harley sharply.

No reply.

'Come, I shall find out, you know. Clarence died only recently, and I am a friend of his brother, Sir George.'

'I lied,' said Hannah miserably. 'I was the housekeeper at Thornton Hall for years and years. Mr Clarence left me five thousand pounds in his will. It has always been my dream to travel and see the world.'

'There was no need to lie to me.'

Hannah raised her eyes. 'There was every need,' she said passionately. 'Servants, my lord, are the most despised class in England. Oh, I have heard the ladies talk about us often in the days when Mrs Clarence used to entertain. Hard as we work, we are regarded as some sort of parasite. The tradesmen and artisans despise us too. They consider the whole servant class lazy and unskilled. You ask me to talk sense to Miss Freemantle. If that young lady realized for a moment she was talking to a servant, then she would not listen to a word I said.'

He looked at her thoughtfully. 'Strange as it may seem, Miss Pym, there was a Pym in my family, a fourth cousin, recently dead, of the Surrey Pyms, the last of the line. I will make you a present. Use your good sense with Miss Freemantle, and you may claim me as kinsman to all who care to listen.'

'It is of no use,' said Hannah. 'My voice . . .'

'What is up with your voice?'

'There is a certain coarseness of accent.'

'My dear Miss Pym, as a lady of your years should know, it is only recently that the ton started ruthlessly shedding their regional accents. I myself went to see a great-aunt in Edinburgh and could not make out a word she was saying. You are over-sensitive on the subject of rank. Banish it from your mind. If it helps, you are now Miss Pym of Surrey.'

'I felt very wicked lying like that,' said Hannah in a small voice. 'Perhaps it is best to tell the truth, and if people are of any worth at all, they will not despise me. Sir George did not. He . . . he took me to Gunter's.'

'Well, there you are. But the world is a wicked and vain place, and there are many misguided people like Emily Freemantle. Think on it. You may use relationship to me as you think fit.' He gave her a charming smile. 'You have perhaps too much character for a gentlewoman and too much concern for others. Why, for example, did you think to bring poor little Mr Fletcher clean linen and a new wig? They were Miss Freemantle's, I assume, and I am also sure she would never have thought of such a thing.'

Hannah put her hands to her face in sudden consternation. 'I have *stolen* from her,' she whispered.

'She has no need of them. Tell her I

commanded you to find something. But you have not answered my question.'

'Oh, dear.' Hannah put down her glass. 'It is this wicked evil drink, my lord. It made me feel so confident, so assured, that it did not dawn on me until now that I was stealing.'

'Tell her first thing in the morning, and if she is enraged, let me know and I will hand everything back, even if I have to rip it off Mr Fletcher. But what was in your mind?'

'I feel Mr Fletcher is a bachelor and has never had anyone to care for him,' said Hannah slowly. 'I do not like that Captain Seaton. I suspect he is an adventurer and after little Mrs Bisley's money. You see, I feel she was married to Mr Bisley and probably very fond of him for a long time. She is one of those ladies who rely totally on a gentleman for their very existence. The captain cleverly moved into the vacuum created by Mr Bisley's death. Mrs Bisley should have more time to mourn. As it was, I think she saw in the disgusting captain a broad shoulder to lean on. Mr Fletcher has a neglected air, neglected in body and spirit. I do not think he has much money, and I do not think anyone has ever cared for him. I thought that perhaps if he were arrayed in clean linen and a good wig, then perhaps . . .'

Her voice trailed away. Lord Harley roared with laughter, his black eyes dancing. 'I' faith, Miss Pym, you are a travelling matchmaker.'

66

'It was the drink,' said Hannah in a hollow voice.

'Poor Mr Fletcher,' said Lord Harley with a grin. 'Into what masterful hands he has fallen. I scrub his back and you make over his clothes. Let well alone, Miss Pym, and heed my advice. Never think for a moment you can alter the course of people's affections. Now we shall have some sobering coffee and go to bed.'

He rang the bell. No one answered its summons. The inn was quiet apart from the roaring of the wind in the chimney.

At last the landlord appeared, looking worried. 'Beg pardon, my lord,' he said, 'but the maids went to their homes in the town as they usually do, along with the waiters, me not having the room to house them here. I got the ostlers to help them through the storm. There's not one here now but me and missus, and she is feeling poorly. I myself will bring you anything you desire.'

'Go to bed, landlord,' said Hannah quickly before Lord Harley could say anything. 'I shall fetch coffee myself. You will need your strength for the morrow.'

'Thank you, mum, but it don't seem fitting.'

'Anything is fitting in such a storm as this. Pray retire,' said Hannah, 'and I shall look at your wife tomorrow and see if she needs help.'

When the landlord had bowed his way out, stammering his thanks, Hannah said, 'I shall

67

fetch the coffee now, my lord.'

'You are no longer a servant, Miss Pym. It appears we must all be our own servants, and it will do us no harm. Lead the way!'

He followed Hannah through a long narrow corridor and then through a green baize door and so to the kitchen of the inn, which was at the back. Here the noise of the storm was worse than ever. He sat at the table and watched as Hannah ground coffee beans and then made a jug of coffee. She was arranging cups on a tray when he said languidly, 'We will drink it here. Are you never tired, Miss Pym?'

'I am fortunate in needing very little sleep,' said Hannah. 'Oh, my lord, what a wonderful day it has been. God is very good.'

'You amaze me, Miss Pym. To my mind we have endured a day which would make most sober people doubt the existence of their Maker.'

'But they have not been starved for adventure, as I,' said Hannah.

They fell into a companionable silence. Lord Harley felt he knew why Sir George, a high stickler if ever there was one, had decided to take the housekeeper to Gunter's. There was something childlike about this Miss Pym, an innocence that was strangely endearing. He thought of Emily Freemantle and his face hardened. What a fool he had been to settle for an arranged marriage. It was not that he did not believe in love. Several of

68

his friends had been fortunate to find it. But he himself never had and was sure now he never would. All he wanted was to settle down with some amiable female and bring up a family. But the next time, he would go about it all the time-honoured way and court and get to know the lady first.

He drained his coffee and thanked Hannah and stood up and stretched his arms above his head. Then he exclaimed, 'I forgot about Mr Fletcher's bath, and there is no one to take it down.'

'I shall help you,' said Hannah.

And so it was. While Mr Fletcher slept curled up in the large bed, Hannah and Lord Harley, on Hannah's instructions, opened the bedroom window, which was fortunately on the leeward side of the inn, and poured out jugs of dirty bath water into the snow. And then Lord Harley lugged the empty bath down to the kitchen, where he left it propped against the back door.

Hannah went to her own room, washed in now cold water, changed into a voluminous night-gown, tied her nightcap under her chin, and crept into bed beside Emily.

Lord Harley was right, she thought sleepily, there was no need to interfere. But Emily was so beautiful and he was so handsome and Emily's parents would be overjoyed if they were to marry after all and that silly Miss Cudlipp would be confounded.

And, still making plans in her head, Hannah fell asleep.

4

Snow had fallen, snow on snow,
Snow on snow,
In the bleak mid-winter,
Long ago.

Christina Rossetti

Hannah awoke at six o'clock, climbed out of bed and drew back the curtains. She could see nothing but a sort of raging white wilderness. She washed and dressed and then raked out the fire and lighted it. If Emily wanted hot water to wash herself, then she would need to fetch it from the kitchen. Hannah was sure none of the servants would be able to manage to get to work that day.

She went down to the kitchen. Mrs Silvers was sitting at the table wearing a night-gown, a wrapper, and a huge red nightcap. Her nose was red and her eyes watery.

'Oh, Miss Pym,' she said. 'I do feel mortal bad.'

'Then you must go to bed,' said Hannah briskly. 'Where is your husband?'

'Out at the stables, rousing the post-boys. They sleeps over the stables.'

'Good,' said Hannah, relieved to find that there was some help. She looked around her. The soiled linen lay piled up in a basket in the corner, but the fire was blazing brightly. 'Please do go to bed, Mrs Silvers,' she urged, 'or we shall all catch your cold. We can all make shift for ourselves.' Her eyes gleamed green with excitement. 'It is an adventure for me.'

Mrs Silvers went reluctantly and Hannah set to work, filling a huge copper with water from the scullery pump and hanging it on a hook over the fire. She found a bar of washing soap and began to shave flakes off it for the wash. There was a container of chicken dung in the scullery, so useful for whitening yellow linen, but Hannah did not think she could bear the smell of it so early in the day. After she had put the clothes on to boil, she made herself a cup of hot chocolate, drank it and then ran up the stairs and roused Emily.

'It is still darkness,' moaned Emily. 'What's to do?'

'The servants went home last night and are not able to return this day because of the ferocity of the storm. You must rouse yourself and help me prepare breakfast.'

'I!' said Emily aghast. 'I, work in a common inn kitchen? No, I thank you. I would rather starve.' She pulled the blankets over her head.

'In that case you will starve!' said Hannah. 'If you are not prepared to work, then you will

71

not be allowed to eat.' She went out and slammed the door behind her.

Lord Harley heard the indomitable Hannah rousing Mrs Bradley and Mrs Bisley. He heard her tell them that there were no servants and that she was in need of help. He picked up his watch and looked at it by the light of the rushlight beside his bed. Seven o'clock. He groaned. But she had the right of it. Everyone must help. He swung his long legs out of bed and then twisted around and looked at the sleeping Mr Fletcher. The lawyer lay calmly asleep. His face looked younger with the lines smoothed away. Lord Harley decided to leave him. Wouldn't be of much help anyway, he thought.

Emily did not go back to sleep. At first she felt tearful. Here she was in a strange inn with that monster somewhere about and she was expected to work like a common servant. It was too bad.

Then she heard Mrs Bradley's voice from the corridor. 'Right you are, Miss Pym, m'dear. Just get my duds on and I'll be with you in a trice.' And then the sleepy voice of Mrs Bisley: 'I shall be there, too, Miss Pym. Give me but twenty minutes.'

The beginnings of an awakening conscience stabbed at Emily. She got out of bed and studied the little amount of cold water left in the cans on the toilet table. She rang the bell and waited. Back down in the kitchen,

Hannah looked up at the swinging bell and tightened her lips. Miss Freemantle would soon find there was no one to wait on her.

Emily washed herself as best she could and brushed her short hair till it shone. She noticed all her clothes had been hung away but assumed the servants had done it while she was asleep. She lifted out a blue kerseymere wool gown. It was high-waisted with a high neck and long sleeves. She put on two petticoats and woollen stockings and half-boots before putting the dress on.

Emily pushed open the door and went into the dining-room. It was cold and dark. She went through to the coffee room. A fire was blazing brightly. She shivered and went to stand in front of it.

The door of the coffee room opened. Lord Ranger Harley came in and stood for a moment watching Emily.

She was standing looking into the flames, one little booted foot on the fender. Then, as if conscious of his gaze, she slowly turned and looked at him, her eyes widening with fear.

'Miss Freemantle,' he said coldly, 'before you start to scream or indulge in any further stupid behaviour, let me make one thing very plain: having met you, I would not marry you if you were the last woman on earth.'

The fear left her eyes and she looked at him in ludicrous amazement. 'You are . . . you are sure?'

'Of course, you widgeon. What man of any sophistication and breeding would want a silly little schoolgirl?'

Her eyes flashed. 'I am out of the schoolroom this age, sir!'

'But your behaviour is not. Where is the excellent Miss Pym?'

'I believe she is in the kitchen.'

'And in need of help?'

'So I believe. But I do not see why—'

'Then shall we join her?'

Emily had been about to say she did not see why she, a lady, should be expected to work in an inn kitchen, but something told her that Lord Harley would despise her further for that remark. Never in her short life had anyone ever despised or disliked Emily. She had been cosseted and feted and petted from the day she was born.

'I do not know where the kitchen is,' she said.

'But I do. Follow me.'

Emily reluctantly followed him through to the kitchen. Hannah was cutting slices of bacon, and Mrs Bisley was frying sausages. Mrs Bradley was out in the scullery, scrubbing the boiled clothes on a washboard.

'More help here,' said Lord Harley. 'What would you like us to do?'

'Lay the table,' said Hannah promptly, 'and then rouse the other guests. They cannot drift down to meals just when they feel like it.'

'Where is a tray for the dishes?' asked Emily, looking helplessly around.

'We'll all dine at the kitchen table,' said Hannah.

All in that moment, Emily hated Hannah Pym. This woman was determined to humiliate her. Emily Freemantle being asked to dine in the kitchen!

'Stop dreaming,' ordered Lord Harley. 'Help me with the plates.'

Hannah handed slices of bacon to Mrs Bisley to put in the pan and watched Lord Harley and Emily out of the corner of her inquisitive eyes. Emily was slamming plates down on the table in a sulky way and Lord Harley was paying no heed to her whatsoever.

Hannah swung open the heavy door of the oven in the wall beside the fire and brought out a tray of hot rolls. She said to Lord Harley, 'If I could trouble you to rouse the other guests.'

Lord Harley grinned at her. 'I'll have trouble with Seaton. The commoner these fellows are, the more they expect to be waited on.'

Emily flushed with mortification, thinking the remark was directed at her.

The rest of the guests, the coachman and guard gradually came in one by one, all still in their undress and yawning and grumbling. The one exception was Mr Fletcher. He looked a new man, thought Hannah with satisfaction.

The wig looked very fine and neat and the whiteness of his shirt and neckcloth was dazzling. His black coat and breeches looked refurbished because Lord Harley had ruthlessly brushed them after he had finished brushing his own clothes.

Hannah pushed Mrs Bisley into a seat and made sure Mr Fletcher was placed next to her. The captain, in a large night-gown with showy frills of cotton lace and a dirty dressing-gown and Kilmarnock nightcap, glowered at Mr Fletcher from the other end of the table. The landlord came in shivering with cold, and looked first amazed and then gratified when Hannah told him to take a seat and served him with breakfast and small beer.

Lord Harley watched Hannah with admiration as she served everyone in record time and then sat down herself, consumed a great quantity of bacon and eggs at amazing speed, and then started to load up a tray to take to Mrs Silvers' bedchamber.

When breakfast was over, Hannah returned to say that as the circumstances were unusual, she would appreciate any help the gentlemen had to offer in clearing up. Emily was about to say that *she* had done enough, but Captain Seaton began to bluster that he was a gentleman and would not soil his hands with women's dirty work. Anxious not to be associated with the captain in the public mind, Emily stood about, hoping she looked willing and hoping at the same time that Hannah would not ask her to do anything.

The coachman, who divulged that his name was Old Tom, or, rather, that that was what everyone on the road called him, said cheerfully that if Hannah put some bits and pieces of food together, along with some ale, he would take it out to the post-boys. Assured by him that the post-boys were snug enough from the storm before the tack-room fire, Hannah set about preparing a tray for them. Ignored, the captain got sulkily to his feet. 'Come along, Mrs Bisley,' he growled. But to his mortification, Lizzie did not seem to hear him. She was tying one of the waiters' aprons around Mr Fletcher's waist, the little lawyer having said he would be glad to help with the dirty dishes.

Mrs Bradley went off to get her basket of medicines to find something to ease Mrs Silvers' cold.

Lord Harley rounded up the rest of the men and said to Hannah's relief that a path to the outside privvy must be dug through the snow, 'for no one surely expects these excellent ladies to empty chamber-pots, and if any of you have used that utensil during the night, then I suggest you carry it down and empty it yourself.'

Emily turned as red as fire. She had been about to nip up to the bedchamber to make use of the chamber-pot but now she could not, for that would mean carrying the nasty thing down in full view of everyone. No one cared about her predicament, she thought tearfully, quite forgetting that no one could possibly know.

The guard, who was called Jim Feathers, and the two outside passengers, Mr Burridge and Mr Hendry, followed Lord Harley outside to find shovels to start digging. Mr Fletcher and Lizzie Bisley were out in the scullery washing dishes.

'Now dinner,' said Hannah. 'There is a pot of stock here, and soup would be a great thing to begin. Miss Freemantle, if you would be so good as to clean the vegetables.'

'I don't know how,' said Emily.

'For a start, here are carrots. You scrape them, so, and then cut them into slices, and when you have finished that, I shall give you the onions.'

Emily felt too intimidated to protest. Lord Harley's remark about not wanting her hurt the more she thought about it. There was no Miss Cudlipp to whisper in her ear that he really did not mean it. And if he returned to the kitchen and found her rebelling, she knew his contempt for her would be awful. He could not really be aristocratic, thought Emily, ferociously chopping carrots. There must be common blood in the Harleys. Aristocrats did not dig snow to clear a path to the privy. Gently born people hardly ever mentioned the

78

place, and if they did, they referred to it as the 'necessary house'.

But when Lord Harley came in, stamping snow from his boots, and said the path was clear, Emily slipped gratefully out of the kitchen and fought her way through the storm to the Jericho in the garden, suddenly grateful she had managed to avoid the humiliation of the chamber-pot. She came back to the kitchen brushing snow from her dress, her cheeks pink with the cold.

'Onions, Miss Freemantle,' said Hannah, putting the offensive, nasty things down on the table. Emily saw a flash of amusement light up Lord Harley's eyes and bent to her work. But while she chopped onions, occasionally rubbing her streaming eyes with a handkerchief, she began to feel a glow of satisfaction. Yes, she had behaved badly by running away, but her doting parents would forgive all when they heard how she had been used. And what stories she would have to tell Miss Cudlipp! She could see Miss Cudlipp's rather sheeplike face looking at her in amazed admiration. 'Come along, Miss Freemantle,' came the hated Miss Pym's voice, 'don't take all day.' Lord Harley grinned and left.

Mr Fletcher was polishing dishes in the scullery and admiring the tender white nape of Lizzie Bisley's neck as she bent over the sink. She turned to hand him another dish and Mr Fletcher, with a little spurt of gladness,

79

noticed the fine network of wrinkles at her eyes. He had thought her much younger than he.

'I could not help but notice you are in mourning and you did say something about having been recently bereaved,' said Mr Fletcher. 'When did your husband. . . er . . . pass on?'

'Eight months ago,' said Lizzie. 'I miss him sore.'

'What did he do?'

'He was a lawyer.'

'Indeed!' Mr Fletcher furrowed his brow. Bisley. Then his face cleared. 'Not John Bisley of Bisley, Rochester & Bisley.'

'The same,' said Lizzie, turning her back on the sink and leaning against it.

'He was a very successful lawyer,' said Mr Fletcher wistfully. 'I, too, am a lawyer, Mrs Bisley, but have not had any success at all. That is why I am going to Exeter, to try my luck there.'

'Do you know anyone in Exeter?'

'Yes, an old school friend. He is in practice in the town. He said he could put some bits and pieces my way.'

Lizzie looked at his tired, sensitive face. 'I am sure you will have better luck in Exeter. And do call on us after we are married.'

'Never!' said Mr Fletcher passionately, and then turned red and twisted the dishcloth in his hands.

Lizzie turned back to the sink and began to attack the plates as if they were personal enemies while Mr Fletcher looked miserably at her slim back.

'I should not have said that. Please forgive me.' Mr Fletcher waited anxiously.

Lizzie slowly turned around. 'Very well, you are forgiven.'

'What think you of our Miss Pym?' asked Mr Fletcher, all eagerness to avoid painful subjects.

'She makes me want to laugh,' said Lizzie with a smile, 'and that is unusual these days. She has those funny eyes and that odd way of looking down her nose. I think she must have been used at one time to managing a large household. She is monstrous efficient.'

They fell to discussing the other members of the party, with the notable exception of Captain Seaton. Out in the kitchen, Hannah was aware the couple were taking a very long time to wash the dishes and was pleased.

She herself was busy hoisting a leg of mutton on to the clockwork spit. She was glad the spit was operated by clockwork. She had a sentimental streak about animals and was always sorry for the dogs when she saw them in their cages turning spits. She saw Emily edging toward the kitchen door, and determined that she must not leave. A little housewifery was the way to a man's heart.

'I would now like you to make some tartlets

81

for dinner, Miss Freemantle,' said Hannah.

'I do not know how to,' said Emily loftily. 'I am used to servants doing all menial work for me.'

'As I am,' said Hannah pleasantly, 'but you must admit the circumstances are extraordinary. There is a recipe here'—she held out a sheet of paper—'for jam tartlets. Very simple. You just follow the instructions and measure out the ingredients. Come. I will show you what to do.'

Emily sighed loudly but returned to the kitchen table. Under Hannah's instructions, she mixed the ingredients for the pastry and made little cases in a baking pan, filled the cases with strawberry jam, and put little crosses of pastry across the top of each.

The storm howled outside. The kitchen fire blazed merrily. The air was full of the smells of cooking. For the first time in her life, Emily felt a sense of achievement as Hannah opened the oven and put those precious tartlets inside.

'And now?' asked Emily.

Hannah smiled. 'And now I think you may repair to the coffee room and have a rest.'

Perversely, Emily was reluctant to leave. The conversation in the scullery had ceased. Lizzie Bisley was singing 'Sweet Lass of Richmond Hill' in a tuneless soprano, and then Mr Fletcher joined in in a light tenor.

'Tartlets on their own are not very much for

dessert,' Emily said. 'Can I try something else?'

'There is fruit-cake,' said Hannah. 'Gentlemen love rich fruit-cake, but I fear that might be beyond your powers.'

'But you could show me?'

'Oh, yes.'

'May we try?'

How very pretty she was, thought Hannah, when whe was like this, all flushed and happy and unselfconscious.

Together they looked out dried fruit and flour and butter and eggs, cream of tartar and baking soda. Hannah took turns at beating the cake because Emily laughed and said her wrists were aching. How excited Emily was when the rich mixture was finally loaded into a round tin. She had forgotten about Lord Harley, about the storm. There was no way she was going to leave that kitchen until the results of her labours came out of the oven.

Hannah set her to grinding coffee beans to make coffee. Mrs Bisley and Mr Fletcher came into the kitchen and said they were going to tidy up the bedchambers and Hannah smiled on them in a maternal way. Lord Harley entered the kitchen with Mr Hendry and Mr Burridge but Hannah shooed them out, saying the ladies were too busy working, and Lord Harley looked at Emily with a flicker of amazement in his black eyes.

Lizzie and Mr Fletcher had to go through

the coffee room to get upstairs to the bedchambers. In front of the coffee-room fire sat Captain Seaton, a glass of brandy in front of him.

'Oh, there you are,' he cried when he saw Lizzie, but his face darkened as he saw the little lawyer behind her.

'We cannot stay,' said Lizzie hurriedly. 'We must do the bedchambers.'

'Do the . . . ? You sit down here, Mrs Bisley. It is time we had a talk. Let that poor fellow there act as chambermaid if he wishes.'

'Take that back,' shouted Mr Fletcher, fists swinging. Lizzie sprang between them. 'Please go . . . for me,' she pleaded with the lawyer. 'I shall join you shortly.' Mr Fletcher reluctantly withdrew.

'Sit down, my sweet,' cajoled the captain. 'We have hardly had time to talk.'

'There is work to do,' said Lizzie. How gross and common the captain seemed. How could she ever have leaned on him for support? She had met him a month before by chance at the home of a friend. He had been low-voiced and courteous then in a sort of bluff way. He had seemed a tower of strength. The fact was that, much as Lizzie was convinced she had adored the late Mr Bisley, the man had been a household bully, not allowing her an idea of her own or any independence whatsoever. His death had left her alone and helpless, not really knowing

84

who she was. The captain had seemed so masculine, so confident, so prepared to take all arrangements for living out of her hands.

'Let the others do it,' the captain was saying. 'This bent-nosed spinster is common enough. She don't mind. But a lady like you . . .'

'Lord Harley does not mind dirtying his hands,' said Lizzie, her voice trembling, for she had not been in the way of speaking up for herself or indeed of contradicting anyone whatsoever.

'That's different,' blustered the captain. 'He's amusing hisself at the moment. Another day and he'll have you waiting on him hand and foot. I command you to sit down here with me.'

Lizzie slowly moved forward and then stopped still.

'No,' she said quietly, 'we must all help. You have no right, sir, to command me to do anything.'

'I am your fiancé, madam, I'll have you know.'

'We were never officially engaged,' said Lizzie sadly. How had it all come about? He had suggested this journey to Exeter. He had said he had friends and family there. But he had made her promise not to tell her friends. Why? And why had she done such a stupid thing? 'Because he ordered you,' said a voice in her head, 'and all your life you have obeyed orders without question.'

'We will talk later,' said Lizzie, her voice slightly squeaky with fright, 'but I am leaving you now.' And she darted from the room.

She ran lightly upstairs and found Mr Fletcher in one of the bedrooms, raking out the fire.

She hesitated in the doorway. He stood up and smiled at her with simple affection. She dreaded his asking her questions but braced herself for them.

Instead, he said mildly, 'We will make up the fires this once, I think, and then announce at dinner that each must see to their own fires while the storm lasts. But there is no need for both of us to dirty our hands. Perhaps if you start to make the beds. . .?'

Lizzie agreed eagerly and was disappointed when the bulk of Mrs Bradley loomed in the doorway offering to help.

With the exception of Captain Seaton, who had done nothing, they all sat down to dinner at four o'clock in the afternoon feeling like brave adventurers. The men and Lord Harley had chopped wood and dug paths in the snow to the stable and to the front of the inn. All were tired from their exertions. Emily nursed burnt fingers. She had been so anxious to take that cake out of the oven herself that she had burnt her fingers on the knob of the oven door.

It was a simple dinner with no extra side

dishes. There was soup to begin with, roast mutton, vegetables and potatoes as a main course, and Emily's tartlets and the cake splendidly iced to make do for dessert.

The men praised Emily the most and Emily took it all as her due, forgetting Hannah had done most of the work. Once more, she was where she felt she belonged, the centre of attention. Normally, she would have drunk lemonade, but everyone was drinking fortified French wine—the English merchants strengthening wine with brandy. She began to talk about her adventures, about running away from home, at first frankly and then, as the wine went to her head, she began to brag.

It was too much for Mr Fletcher. Emily had reached the point in her narrative when she had taken over the whole running of the inn single-handed. 'Now, now,' he chided, 'you are going too far, Miss Freemantle. You must admit Miss Pym organized the inside work and Lord Harley arranged all the outside work. Mrs Bisley here has been washing dishes and making beds and cleaning the bed-chambers for all of you.'

Stopped in mid-flight, Emily looked at him tipsily and then her eyes narrowed.

'That looks very much like my wig,' she said. 'How did you come by it?'

'I gave it to him,' said Hannah, cursing inwardly. 'You have no need of men's clothes, my child.'

'Just helping out the poor,' jeered Captain Seaton.

Mr Fletcher leaped to his feet, his face scarlet. He tore off the wig, walked round the table, and laid it in front of Emily, and, looking like an angry fledgling with his short-cropped hair, he stalked out of the room.

Emily rounded on Hannah. 'You had no right to *steal* from me,' she snapped.

'I meant to discuss the matter with you,' said Hannah, standing her ground, 'but I forgot.'

'What di'ye think of your pauper lawyer now, Mrs Bisley?' laughed the captain. 'Can't even afford a decent wig.'

Lizzie burst into tears and ran from the table.

There was a silence and then Lord Harley's voice, dripping ice, said contemptuously, 'You silly goose. How dare you humiliate poor Mr Fletcher so? You could have had a word with him in private. But not you. You were bragging and bragging and puffing yourself up and he rightly pointed out that everyone else had been working much harder. I'll buy the poxy wig from you. How much?'

Emily looked at him white-faced. She could have stood his contempt, for she had cast him in the role of villain, but Old Tom the coachman was shaking his head at her in a reproachful way, and cozy and fat Mrs Bradley was actually looking at her with dislike. Her only ally was the captain, and who wanted an ally like that?

'I hate you all!' she shouted. Hannah watched as she stumbled from the table and then from the room.

'Excuse me,' she said. 'Landlord, I shall leave you to serve the port.'

She went up to Lizzie's room and knocked softly on the door. There was no reply. After a moment's hesitation, she went in. The room was empty. She stood for a moment, baffled, and then went to the room Mr Fletcher shared with Lord Harley and leaned her ear against the door. She could hear Lizzie crying and the low sound of Mr Fletcher's voice comforting her.

Perhaps it was the best thing that could happen, she thought. But what a silly child Emily is. I will never be able to make a match for her. And yet I wish Lord Harley could have seen her when she was alone with me in the kitchen. So natural. So charming. I will not go to her. She deserves to suffer a little.

She went back downstairs and determinedly began to talk of every subject she could think of to keep the conversation going.

Up in the Blue Room, Emily was putting on a warm cloak and a felt hat and gloves. Bagshot was a town. There was bound to be another hostelry, and surely the storm had abated. All she had to do was walk a little way, find another inn, and send them to collect the trunks.

Glad only that the rest of the travellers were still in the kitchen and not in the dining-room, she made her way softly to the main door of the inn.

Gently she opened it and then closed it softly behind her. She could hear the scream of the wind, but it had stopped snowing and a path had been shovelled through the courtyard to the gate.

She left the shelter for the high-walled courtyard and turned right.

And then the full force of the blown snow driven by the wind struck her. It was as if some white monster had been lying in wait for her, and then pounced. In the swinging light of the lantern over the arch to the courtyard, she could see long blown fingers of snow reaching out to her just before she was engulfed in a stunning white maelstrom.

5

Whoe'er has travell'd life's dull round,
Where'er his stages may have been,
May sigh to think he still has found
His warmest welcome at an inn.

William Shenstone

Emily gasped and wheeled about, turning her back to the driving wind and snow and raising the hood of her cloak over her head. A craven voice inside her was telling her to go back, but a stronger voice urged her on. There must be some other hostelry quite near.

She turned around and put her head down and struggled forward into the raging darkness. Emily was typically English in that the occasional erratic savagery of the climate took her by surprise. This could not be England, she thought, this dismal arctic waste, this lower ring of purgatory. Soon the wind would drop and the stars would twinkle.

A snow-drift loomed up in front of her on the road and she waded right into it. She battled her way back out and shielded her eyes. Now any form of habitation would do. But there was nothing but the high eldritch screech of the wind and the blowing, stinging, blinding snow. No yellow candlelight flickered to mark even the lowest cottage.

She was very, very cold and becoming more frightened by the minute. She was about to turn and retreat the way she had come when she saw a light in front of her, flickering erratically in the dark.

She forged towards it and almost collided with a man carrying a lantern. 'Oh, sir!' cried Emily. 'Where is the nearest inn?'

He held the lantern high and Emily saw a rough uncouth face and a mouthful of broken teeth. 'Well, what 'ave we 'ere?' said the man.

'Nothing, nothing,' said Emily, suddenly frightened. She backed a pace. He seized the front of her cloak and dragged her up against him. 'Give us a kiss,' he said.

His horrible breath fanned her face. With a whimper of pure terror, she kicked him on the shins and, as he fell back, she ran past him, struggling through drifts, plunging through them, heading ever farther away from the inn.

*   *   *

Lizzie Bisley came back into the kitchen followed by Mr Fletcher, who was wearing his old wig. Emily's wig still lay by her place.

Hannah noticed Lizzie's eyes were red from crying and wondered whether she had been crying over Mr Fletcher's humiliation or her own predicament. Probably both, thought Hannah, sharply ordering Mr Burridge to pass the port.

Captain Seaton opened his mouth to say something, caught Lord Harley's eye, and closed it again. Lizzie and Mr Fletcher were talking in low whispers. Something would have to be done about that lawyer fellow, thought the captain. When he had first been introduced to Lizzie, he felt he had discovered a gold mine. Here was a rich widow, frail and feminine, looking for a strong man. He had no intention of letting such a prize be snatched from him.

Hannah rose from the table. She was suddenly anxious about Emily. She felt the girl had had long enough to come to her senses. Excusing herself, she went up to the bed-chamber. There was no Emily, but her trunks were still there. Hannah was just about to go downstairs again when she decided to look in the wardrobe. She recognized Emily's missing cloak almost immediately. She had noticed it particularly when she had hung it away the evening before. It was of thick wool and lined with fur.

Beginning to feel alarmed, she ran lightly down to the kitchen. 'I fear Miss Freemantle has gone out.'

'Gone out!' demanded Lord Harley. 'You cannot mean she has gone out in this storm.'

'I am very much afraid so,' said Hannah. 'We had better organize a search party.'

Lord Harley rose to his feet. 'No need to risk everyone else's lives. I will go myself, and

93

should I need help, I will get the post-boys and the rest of you men.'

He went upstairs and put on his greatcoat and hat and then went back down and collected a lantern from the landlord.

He saw the faint tracks of Emily's feet in the snow that lay in the sheltered courtyard. Just at the gate where the great arch still provided shelter, he noticed the footprints turning off to the right.

So Emily had not gone out to find another inn, as he had first thought. The way to the right headed straight into the countryside, for the Nag's Head was on the very edge of the town.

He cursed as the full force of the wind took him. He was becoming increasingly worried. The cold was bitter. If she had tumbled into a snow-drift, he would not find her until daylight.

'Miss Freemantle!' he shouted. But the roaring wind drowned his voice. He strode on, waving the lantern and shouting with all his might. He waded through a drift that came up to his waist. How on earth had the spoilt Emily managed through that? He had walked about a mile and was becoming hoarse with shouting when suddenly the wind dropped, roaring away across the countryside, leaving a moon-washed landscape of dazzling snow pitted with blue and black shadows. And then, far ahead, on a straight stretch of snow-covered road, he thought he saw a figure. He quickened his pace. Something made him remain silent, as if he knew that Emily might run off into the fields if she thought she was being pursued.

Emily was at the end of her tether. She felt like a sodden, freezing mass of exhausted misery. Only the thought of the long walk back to the inn and the humiliation that awaited her spurred her on, although she had begun to stagger from weariness. And then the wind dropped and she stood for a moment shivering, her eyes scanning the white landscape. For the first time, she realized she had taken the wrong direction. That was why no light had shone near the road. She gave a choked sob. There was nothing for it. She turned about. And then she saw the dark figure of a man striding towards her, the lantern bobbing.

It was the ruffian! He had come back for her.

Emily swerved off the road and into a small wood, running and stumbling and falling, dragging herself up only to run headlong again.

And then a hand seized her shoulder. 'I have money,' she screamed. 'Do not hurt me. You may have it all. Please do not hurt me.'

'I would like to wring your neck,' said Lord Harley's voice. He turned her round and shone the lantern in her face.

'Oh, it's you,' said Emily and burst into tears.

He watched her impatiently and then put an arm round her and gave her a gentle shake. 'Rally, Miss Freemantle. Rally! I fear this is only a lull in the storm. We'd best get back as soon as possible.'

'I c-can't go back,' said Emily. 'I am so ashamed.'

'You were tipsy and tactless,' he said. 'Nothing out of the common way. Come along, Miss Freemantle. I do not want to present your parents with a block of ice as a daughter. Did you plan to walk all the way to London?'

'No, I was looking for another inn. I went the wrong way and there was this ruffian, and he . . . he . . .'

'He what?'

'He tried to kiss me.'

'You are on Bagshot Heath and lucky to be alive. Come along.'

His arm still around her shoulders, he urged her towards the road. He then put a strong arm about her waist and, almost lifting her from the ground, hurried her along.

He was amazed to feel his senses quickening at that contact and thought it absurd that such a thing should happen when he was cold and tired. But he held her closer to the warmth of his body. With a great almighty roar, the wind came hurtling down

96

the road towards them and enveloped them in a whirling white snowstorm. Now it was not only blowing snow but falling snow they had to contend with.

They reached one of the largest snow-drifts on the road. He stopped and held the lantern high, looking for the passage he had made in it earlier, and the light fell on Mrs Bradley's anguished face. And that was all that could be seen of Mrs Bradley, for the rest of her was buried in the drift.

He left Emily and went forward and began to scoop the snow away from Mrs Bradley with his hands. 'I come out with me basket of medicines,' said Mrs Bradley, 'for to see if I could find Miss Freemantle, and I got so frit in the snow-drift, I couldn't move.'

'You can move now,' said Lord Harley sharply. 'You ladies walk behind me and keep close. We are nearly at the inn.'

When Emily at last saw the faint glow of the lamp swinging outside the inn courtyard, she experienced such a feeling of relief it almost warmed her. They turned into the courtyard to be met by an expedition party: the landlord, the guard, the coachman, Mr Fletcher, and the two outsiders, Mr Hendry and Mr Burridge, carrying staves and lanterns.

Hannah Pym, waiting on the steps like a field marshal surveying his troops, hustled Emily and Mrs Bradley into the coffee room, where a large fire was blazing. Hannah's shrewd eyes studied them. Emily, for all her bad experience, was young and strong and would come about. Mrs Bradley was another matter. She was a bluish-white colour and her breathing was ragged.

'Miss Freemantle, go to our room and change into dry clothes and then come down to the kitchen,' ordered Hannah. She turned to Lizzie. 'Fetch Mrs Bradley's night-dress and wrapper and clean towels and bring them down to the kitchen. Mr Burridge and Mr Hendry, if you please, I need help in the kitchen to fill a bath.'

Mrs Bradley sat down by the kitchen table and drank a glass of brandy. Hannah had had to prise her precious basket from her wrist. A large copper pan and two kettles were already steaming on the fire.

'Put the bath on the floor in front of the kitchen fire,' Hannah ordered the men, 'and help me fill it.'

Mrs Bradley drank brandy and shivered and watched curiously, thinking they must be getting water ready for a mammoth wash.

Lizzie entered with the night-things and towels. Emily appeared and was offered brandy. She did not know why Hannah had ordered her to the kitchen. Surely after such an ordeal, she should be allowed to go to sleep.

'Right,' said Hannah, hands on hips. 'Off you go, gentlemen, and I thank you.' She closed and locked the door behind them and then said to Mrs Bradley, 'Off with those wet clothes and in the bath.'

'Me!' Mrs Bradley's eyes were childlike with wonder. 'I don't take no baths.'

'I know,' said Hannah, wrinkling her nose. 'But this is not an ordinary bath, this is a medicinal bath, Mrs Bradley, as recommended by Queen Charlotte's physician.'

'But I can't strip down to me buffs in front of you ladies.'

'You may keep on your shift,' said Hannah, rightly thinking that that garment could do with a wash as well. Her eyes fell on Emily and gleamed with a green light. 'Miss Freemantle, I suggest you go and do what's right and then return and help me and Mrs Bisley.'

'What's right?' echoed Emily faintly.

'Work it out for yourself. Examine your conscience.'

Emily wearily left the kitchen. What did that fiend of a woman want her to do?

She went slowly up to her room, determined to climb into that soft bed and sink into oblivion. But on the bed was her wig, the one that had caused all the trouble. There was that stab of conscience, sharp and acute. She was too tired to worry about pride. She went down to the coffee room. The men, with the exception of the coachman and Captain Seaton, who were in the tap, were grouped around the fire. Lord Harley was standing, mixing a bowl of punch. He was grating lemons but stopped, looking curiously at Emily as she came into the room. Women's dress of the year 1800 was not designed for warmth. Emily had only one wool gown. All her other dresses followed the dictates of fashion, namely, that everything should be flimsy and light enough to be rolled up and put in a pocket. She was wearing a gown of white muslin, cut low, and looped over the arm on the left to disclose one leg in a salmon-coloured silk stocking. It was quite a delicious leg, mused Lord Harley. Over her shoulders, she wore a Norfolk shawl, and in one hand, she carried the wig. She went straight to Mr Fletcher and said in a low voice, 'I am most sorry for having caused you such embarrassment. I have no need of this wig and should never have had it in the first place. Be so good as to accept it as a present and also to accept my heartfelt apologies.'

'Well, I . . . I . . .' Mr Fletcher looked around for help.

'A charming gesture, if I may say so,' said Lord Harley.

'Yes,' said Mr Fletcher, and, sensitive creature that he was, suddenly realized the effort the apology must have cost Emily. 'I am delighted to accept your gift, Miss Freemantle,' he said, executing a low bow. 'Not only is it an excellent wig and much finer than anything I could afford, but when I wear it, I shall have the joy of remembering your pretty face.'

He took the wig. 'Stay and have some punch with us,' said Lord Harley.

'No, I thank you,' said Emily faintly. 'Miss Pym wants me in the kitchen.'

When she had gone, Lord Harley finished making the punch, urged the others to help themselves, and went through to the kitchen at the back and knocked on the door. Hannah opened it an inch. 'Lord Harley?'

'A word, if you please,' said Lord Harley.

Hannah opened the door slightly more and slid through like an eel so that his lordship should not catch any glimpse of Mrs Bradley in her bath.

'I wish to speak to you about Miss Freemantle,' he said. 'She is exhausted and has had quite an ordeal. I think you should send her to bed.'

'She is young and robust,' said Hannah. 'I have dealt with many young housemaids, you know.'

'But we are talking about a *lady!*'

'Ho, yes,' said Hannah, squinting down her nose. 'Well, let me tell you, my lord, and this may come as a surprise, but servants can be every bit as frail and sensitive as their betters, but the reason they rarely go into declines or have the vapours is because they just have to get on with life. Miss Freemantle has been pampered enough. This is a blessed opportunity to lick her into shape.'

'If she falls ill,' he said grimly, 'I must hold you responsible.'

'Do that,' said Hannah, grinning at him suddenly, and then slipped into the kitchen again.

'Now, Mrs Bradley,' said Hannah. 'Out of the bath and into your night-gown.' She picked up a huge huckaback towel and held it out.

'Right you are, m'dear,' said Mrs Bradley. She put both chubby hands on either side of the tin bath and heaved. Nothing happened. She stared up at Hannah, her eyes wide with consternation. 'I be *stuck,*' she moaned.

'Fustian,' said Hannah. 'Miss Freemantle, take one of her hands and pull at the same time as I take the other.'

Both tugged mightily, but the only result was a wave of dirty bath-water over the floor.

Lizzie added her efforts but to no avail.

'I'll need to get one of the men,' said Hannah.

Mrs Bradley, who up until then had been restored by the warmth of the bath and a quantity of French brandy, turned almost as awful a colour as she had been when she came in out of the storm. 'You will be quite decent,' said Hannah. 'Miss Freemantle, go to the linen press on the first landing and bring a thick sheet to cover her.'

Emily did as she was bid and returned to find Lord Harley waiting outside the kitchen door. 'What on earth is going on?' he asked. 'I've been told to wait here by Miss Pym until called.'

'We are in need of your help,' said Emily. 'Mrs Bradley is s-stuck in the bath.' She began to giggle helplessly, leaning against the kitchen door. Lord Harley began to laugh as well.

The door opened a crack and Hannah's cold eye surveyed the laughing pair. 'Pull yourselves together,' she admonished. 'My lord, be as quick and deft as you can, for Mrs Bradley is sore embarrassed.'

They followed Hannah into the kitchen. Not only Mrs Bradley's body was covered by a sheet but her face as well.

'Give me your hands, Mrs Bradley,' ordered Lord Harley. Two hands appeared from below the sheet. He gave a great heave. The bath tilted and more water flooded on the floor but Mrs Bradley remained stuck fast.

'I am sorry about this,' he said, bending over the coffin-shaped tin bath to examine her more closely. He took off his coat and rolled up his shirt-sleeves and slid his hands into the water under the sheet and then, as a squawk of sheer outrage rose from Mrs Bradley's lips, under her bottom. With one almightly wrench he lifted her clear from the bath and set her down on her feet.

Panting and blushing, Mrs Bradley wrapped the sheet round her ample body.

'Like Venus rising from the foam,' said Lord Harley gently and kissed one plump cheek.

'Oh, go on with you, me lord,' giggled a newly coquettish Mrs Bradley.

Lord Harley grinned, picked up his coat, and strode from the kitchen.

Mrs Bradley submitted docilely, glad her ordeal was soon to be over, as Lizzie and Hannah began to towel her down. Soon she was dressed in her night-gown and wrapper, flushed and rosy.

She moved to the door. 'Wait till I tell my folks I had a lord's hands under me bum,' she said and went out, closing the door behind her.

Emily began to laugh helplessly. Hannah and Lizzie joined in, and still laughing, the three women began to empty the bath and clear up the mess on the floor.

Then Hannah set to brewing a posset for Emily to take to Mrs Silvers, the landlord's wife.

Mrs Silvers was sitting up in bed knitting. As soon as she saw Emily, she sank back against the pillow and groaned. 'I feel so poorly,' she whispered. Emily thought Mrs Silvers looked recovered and had a suspicion that lady was going to make the most of being waited on, but she simply handed her the posset and told her gently to drink it up.

Emily returned to the kitchen to find there were dishes still to be washed and pots to be scrubbed. But she was too tired to protest. Hannah let her work for half an hour and then said, 'You may go to bed now, Miss Freemantle.'

'But both of you must be tired as well,' said Emily. 'We have not been out in a snowstorm. Off with you,' commanded Hannah.

Emily went upstairs. She had left her sodden clothes lying on the floor. She slowly picked them up and arranged them over a couple of straight-backed chairs in front of the fire. Wearily, she made ready for bed. All she wanted to do was sleep and sleep.

But no sooner was her head on the pillow than she felt very wide awake indeed. Images of the evening flashed through her mind: the feel of Lord Harley's strong arm at her waist, how they had stood laughing outside the kitchen door, how sweet Mrs Bradley had looked when he had kissed her. A great roar shook the inn. She climbed from bed and went to the window and drew back the curtains. She could see nothing but whiteness.

She climbed back into bed. She wondered if Miss Pym had learned that Mr Fletcher had accepted that wig. What an odd woman she was. She was surely not a lady, and yet she had an air of authority. Then there was Mrs Bisley. Not only Mr Fletcher but all the men treated little Mrs Bisley with courtesy and kindness.

And she was quite old. But Emily had to admit that Lizzie Bisley with her brown hair and pansy-brown eyes managed to look defenceless and fragile and much younger than her years. What a pity about the gross captain. Emily felt sure Mrs Bisley was making a terrible mistake.

She fell into an uneasy sleep and awoke as Hannah Pym climbed into bed beside her.

'I apologized to Mr Fletcher,' said Emily sleepily, 'and gave him the wig as a present, which he accepted most graciously.'

'I knew you would,' said Hannah.

'Why?' asked Emily.

'Because I have discovered this day,' said Hannah firmly, 'that although you have been badly spoilt, underneath it all, you are a young lady of resource, courage and humour.'

'Really!' said Emily, experiencing a glow of pleasure.

There was no reply. She twisted about and looked at her sleeping partner, but it seemed that Hannah Pym had fallen neatly and quietly asleep.

Along the corridor, Mrs Bradley and Lizzie lay side by side in a big four-poster bed.

Lizzie turned on her side and Mrs Bradley's voice sounded in the darkness. 'Reckon you've made a mistake with that captain, m'dear.'

Lizzie sighed and said faintly, 'I cannot do anything now. I gave my word. Oh, Mrs Bradley, I wish it would snow and snow and snow so that we might never reach Exeter.'

'All it takes is a little courage,' said Mrs Bradley comfortably. 'Now, me, I ain't got none, but if I was you, I would ask that Miss Pym for help. Her could take on a whole battalion of Napoleon's soldiers.'

'My late husband,' said Lizzie, 'was a strong man. He made all the decisions for me. I never even had a thought of my own. But you know how it is. My family were so proud of him. Everyone kept telling me I was lucky to have such a fine upstanding man as a husband, and so . . . and so . . .'

'You felt it downright wicked to think anything else,' said Mrs Bradley. 'Children might ha' helped.'

'Oh, but I have two sons, twins, of twenty-two. They work in the business. I mean, they are both lawyers. Everyone says they are the image of their father.'

'Not comfortable for you. What did they think of the captain?'

'They do not know,' said Lizzie in a low voice. 'Captain Seaton said it was no concern of theirs and that they might be angry at the idea of me remarrying so soon. He arranged everything and I just went along with it.'

'You got a tidy bit o' money then?' asked Mrs Bradley.

'Yes, I am fortunate in being comfortably off.'

'How's that come about? Thought your

dear departed would ha' left most to the sons.'

'There were marriage settlements. I have my own money.'

'And that's what the captain wants, mark my words. Not that they all wants money. That Mr Fletcher would take you if you hadn't a penny.'

'Do you think so?' asked Lizzie, her voice lightening. 'I feel so comfortable with him. He asks me what I think. Most strange in a man.'

'There's still some good'uns around. Now go to sleep, there's a love.'

Lizzie fell almost immediately into a deep sleep and dreamt she was travelling on the stage on a sunny warm day with Mr Fletcher sitting beside her, holding her hand.

In the Red Room, Mr Fletcher cautiously raised himself on one elbow. 'Are you awake, my lord?'

'Only just,' said Lord Harley amiably.

'I think it was noble and generous of Miss Freemantle to present me with that fine wig.'

'It was the least she could do,' said Lord Harley cynically.

'No, I think not. She has obviously led a pampered life and she is so very beautiful, and in my experience beautiful young ladies think their beauty is enough to offer the world. And yet she made her apology with such sincerity and grace.'

'Mark my words, Miss Freemantle was still shocked from her ordeal in the storm. She will no doubt be restored to her spoilt self on the morrow. I wish this storm would blow itself out.'

'I think there is a change in the weather coming. I can feel it in my left leg,' said Mr Fletcher.

'Let's hope your left leg is right. What a day. Running after that stupid female and then having to dislodge Mrs Bradley from the bath.'

'Why, what happened?'

Lord Harley told him and then began to laugh, not over Mrs Bradley's predicament but becaue he remembered how infectious Emily's laughter had been outside the kitchen door.

Mr Fletcher began to laugh as well, until a thud from the next room and the captain's voice roaring, 'Quiet!' effectively reminded him of his worries and his laughter died.

'There is something nasty about that fellow,' said Lord Harley. 'Watch how you go.'

'I shall. I shall indeed. What a gross individual.'

'And I suspect a cruel one,' said Lord Harley slowly. 'Do not let yourself be alone with him.'

'If he tries anything, I shall trounce him,' said Mr Fletcher.

'You cannot trounce a knife in the back,' said Lord Harley.

6

Of all the horrid, hideous notes of woe,
Sadder than owl-songs or the midnight blast
Is that portentous phrase, 'I told you so.'
                                        Lord Byron

Mr Fletcher's leg proved a bad weather-vane.
The storm was raging as viciously as before
when the travellers met in the kitchen. Emily
was subdued. She had put on her wool gown
again after giving it a good brushing, muslin
having proved too cold for even a well-fired
English inn. It was all very well to wear
delicate muslins and silks when there were
gentlemen to charm, but who was there to
charm among this odd assembly? Certainly
not Lord Ranger Harley, unfeeling brute that
he was. He must know she was delicate. He
had seen her faint at the very sound of his
name. Hannah had pointed out to Emily that
her faint was probably due to overexcitement
and lack of food, having noticed that 'Edward'
had eaten nothing on the journey until they
reached Bagshot.

Emily was feeling martyred and rather
enjoying it. She looked at her pink, burnt
fingers with a certain amount of satisfaction.
How her parents would exclaim at her
treatment. There would certainly be no

question of their frail and beautiful daughter marrying such an ogre. But then that old uncomfortable thought crept into her mind. Lord Harley showed no signs of wanting to marry her. As she began to clear away the dirty dishes, she cast him a sidelong look. He was sitting at his ease at the head of the table. He was wearing a black coat with silver buttons and a ruffled shirt. His black hair shone in the lamplight and his black eyes were lazy and amused. Lizzie, too, was helping to clear up. She had collected a heavy pile of dishes. Lord Harley promptly jumped to his feet and took them from her. He never would have thought of doing that for me, sulked Emily, stalking off into the scullery.

'It looks as if we are allocated dishwashing duties this morning,' came Lord Harley's voice behind her. 'I observe you have burnt your fingers. You had best let me wash and you dry.'

'It is nothing,' said Emily mournfully. 'I am become accustomed to pain.'

'Mortification is good for the soul,' he said heartlessly. 'When you return to your pampered life and that chuckle-headed governess of yours, you will appreciate all the cosseting as never before. You will tell your future husband times out of number of your dreadful adventures on this particular journey, for no more adventures will happen to you.'

'And what makes you think that?'

111

demanded Emily, watching him take off his coat and roll up his sleeves.

'You are not the kind to have adventures,' he said. 'You think too much about yourself. People who think of others somehow make for themselves an adventurous life.'

'But I do think of others!' exclaimed Emily, cut to the quick.

He gave her a gentle push aside and lifted a bucket of hot water from the floor and poured it into the sink. 'Who, for instance?'

'For instance,' whispered Emily, 'poor little Mrs Bisley. She must not marry that captain.'

'And how do you think that can be prevented?' Emily's eyes shone. 'You could challenge him to a duel.'

'I do not duel with such as Captain Seaton. In fact, I go to extreme lengths to avoid duels.'

He handed Emily a dish to dry.

'So,' said Emily, rubbing the plate vigorously, 'you are afraid, my lord.'

'What heroes of the corner chimney-seat you ladies are! If you yourselves were in danger of having a yard of cold steel or a bullet through you in the early hours of the morning, it might change your attitude. Besides, I do not wish to seem to brag, but I am an expert shot and a tolerably good swordsman. Although I have been in many battles, strange as it may seem, I do not relish killing, nor, for that matter, should I kill someone in a duel, would I relish having to flee the country.'

'Well, *you* think of something,' said Emily pettishly.

'Intimacy, Miss Freemantle, will work its own charms. I have great hopes of Mr Fletcher.'

'But Mrs Bisley is promised to the captain. It would not be at all convenable for her to give him his marching orders.'

'You are hardly in a position to discuss the conventions. Not for one moment did you spare a thought for my feelings.'

He turned round from the sink and looked at her mockingly. Emily's eyes were round with surprise. 'But you haven't got any!'

'Just because I have decided I have had a lucky escape, Miss Freemantle, I am not devoid of feelings. For example, my poor heart aches for Mrs Bisley . . . so vulnerable, so charming, so feminine . . .'

'And so old,' said Emily waspishly.

He looked at her with amusement and went back to washing dishes. Emily surveyed his elegant back. She had a longing to throw a plate at his head.

She continued her work in grim silence and yet felt almost sorry, although she did not know why, when the dishes and pots were all cleaned and put away.

Hannah, Mrs Bisley and Mrs Bradley were all preparing dinner. 'Why do we not keep town hours?' said Emily. 'We could have a later dinner and not have to start work as soon as breakfast is over.'

'There's nothing else to do,' said Hannah placidly. 'Do you want to help here or will you do the bedchambers?'

'I will do the bedchambers,' said Emily.

'I'll be along to help you soon as I've finished,' said Mrs Bradley.

Emily went upstairs. She started with the Blue Room. Hannah Pym never left anything lying around, and so all Emily had to do was empty out the washing-water, which she did by opening the window and pouring the contents out into the storm. She raked out the hearth and carried the ashes downstairs. Mr Fletcher met her and said he would take the ashes outside to supply some grit for the paths the men were digging.

She went back to the Blue Room and got the fire ready and set for lighting in the evening. Then she went to the Red Room. The bed there was made up and the fire cleaned. All she had to do was dust. Lord Harley's clothes were hung away in the wardrobe. Two books lay beside the bed. She picked one up. It was in ancient Greek and she put it down with an exclamation of disgust. She had been hoping to find a novel she could borrow. There was a miniature beside the bed. She picked it up. The face of a very pretty woman looked out at her. 'So that's your opera dancer,' she said aloud.

'No, not my opera dancer,' said an amused voice from the doorway. 'My mother.'

Emily blushed, feeling like a snooping serving maid. He was leaning against the doorjamb watching her. She was conscious of his masculinity, of a sudden sharp awareness of sexual tension, of the large bed behind her, and of the dead silence created by the muffling snow outside.

'It is fortunately very tidy in here,' she said rather breathlessly. 'I had better check the other rooms.'

She approached the doorway. She had to pass very close to him. Her eyes flew up to meet his, wary and cautious. He raised his hands and she shrank back.

'Fear not, Miss Freemantle,' he mocked. 'My solitaire is coming undone.' He retied the black silk ribbon that confined his thick black hair at the nape of his neck and then smiled at her.

She darted past him and went into a small narrow room next door. Captain Seaton had the luxury of sleeping alone. His room was like a pigsty—clothes thrown here and there, ash spilling out of the fire, water spilled on the floor, and the blankets half pulled off the bed.

'Leave it,' said Lord Harley from behind her. 'Let the pig stew in his own muck.'

'It must be very soul-destroying to be a chambermaid,' said Emily.

'I think a local girl would count herself

115

fortunate to have a job which did not involve work in the scullery.'

'Perhaps. It is all very lowering. You do not seem to mind.'

'I am older than you. In my day . . .' Lord Harley paused, thinking he sounded ancient. 'In my day,' he went on firmly, 'we were expected to do everything a servant could do and better. That applied to the ladies as well. These days, I doubt if the new breed of married lady has ever seen the inside of her own kitchen.'

'I have been in mine—many times,' said Emily proudly.

'To filch cakes from the cook? That is not the same thing. I shall help you with the remaining rooms.'

He saw the rising colour on Emily's face and realized she did not want to be alone with him in any bedroom. The silly wench probably thinks I might rape her, he thought. 'And while we are doing that,' he went on, 'you will help me write a small play for our friends.'

Diverted, Emily exclaimed, 'A play? Why?'

'If we all sit around at dinner and, after dinner, drinking too much, quarrels will break out. Amateur theatricals are just what we need. We need a little play, and one which involves all of us.' He raised an eyebrow at her. 'You, of course, Miss Freemantle, will be the heroine.'

Emily's eyes lit up. 'We could have a play

116

based on the inn. I have run away with my mother, that's Mrs Bisley, and with my old nurse, that's Mrs Bradley, from my wicked uncle . . .'

'And that is I?'

'No, no. Captain Seaton, I think. He descends on the inn and produces a gun, and my brave swain, Jack, wrests it from his hand . . .'

'And who is Jack?'

'Oh, dear, I suppose it will have to be you, my lord, only it would be so much better if you were younger and had golden hair.'

'Like Mr Peregrine Williams?'

'Like . . .? Oh, yes, I suppose so. And the coachman can be the coachman, and the guard, the guard, and Mr Burridge and Mr Hendry can play themselves—passengers, I mean.'

'And what of Mr Fletcher?'

Emily bit her lip. He watched her expressive face with amusement.

Then her face cleared. 'Mr Fletcher can be the family lawyer, of course, and he . . . I have it! He has discovered that the wicked uncle forged Mrs Bisley's late husband's will and that he actually has no longer any power over her because Mrs Bisley has all the money. Mrs Bisley is so grateful that she marries the lawyer and . . .'

'And Miss Emily marries her Jack?'

'Yes, yes, but only for the purposes of the

play,' said Emily.

'You have forgot Miss Pym.'

'So I had. Miss Pym can be the stage manager and find costumes for us.'

'I think I would like everyone to have a part,' said Lord Harley.

'Oh, dear, who can Miss Pym be?'

'She is a respectable lady,' said Lord Harley, 'to whom Captain Seaton once promised marriage, but instead he ruined her after having spent all her savings.'

Emily jumped up and down and clapped her hands. 'Oh, famous! When can we begin to write our play?'

'Just as soon as we have done the bedchambers. We will then go to the kitchen and tell the others.'

Hannah's odd eyes gleamed green when she heard about the proposed play. A bit of fun was what was needed to bring Mrs Bisley out of her worries about her predicament. Besides, what of Lord Harley and Miss Freemantle? Emily's eyes were shining and Lord Harley was looking at her with indulgent amusement.

The landlord, appealed to, produced sheets of paper. Emily was excused from kitchen duties, and she and Lord Harley retreated to the coffee-room hearth. The rest of the travellers, even Captain Seaton, were highly delighted at the idea of the play.

Mr Burridge and Mr Hendry elected to set

up the end of the coffee room as a stage. It was decided that everyone should wear whatever clothes that seemed appropriate for the part.

Emily began to write busily in a clear hand and Lord Harley copied down what she had written on to different sheets of paper. The whole play or playlet was only to last for about twenty minutes. Captain Seaton said he had a gun. He would point it, unloaded, of course, as someone fired a gun off-stage to produce the desired effect. As he wrote busily, Lord Harley wondered if Emily realized that she had written a touching end to the play where brave Jack clasps the heroine in his arms and kisses her. He thought ruefully that she was probably imagining this fellow Peregrine in the role.

Then it was discovered that the coachman could not read and that even Mrs Bradley was going to have difficulty with the words, but that was solved when it was agreed on that they should make up appropriate lines for themselves.

It was a merry dinner with everyone eating and trying to memorize lines and discussing what they would wear. Even Mrs Silvers put in an appearance, saying, despite her rosy cheeks and air of good country health, that she had forced herself from her sick-bed just to see the play.

It was only when the play began that the

exasperated Emily, cast in the role of Lady Gwendoline, realized that her fellow players were determined to play their roles in their own way. Brave Jack was played by Lord Harley as a mincing fop to great effect. The audience of the landlord and his wife were laughing heartily. Then the coachman, elated by his first appearance on the boards, made a long speech about the life of a coachman, the guard told him not to be such an old windbag, the coachman threw up his fists and said he would draw his cork, and Lord Harley, briefly dropping his role of fop, had to separate them. Hannah Pym, remembering the deception of that under-butler, began to berate Captain Seaton in very convincing tones and with such fire and passion that the landlord leaped to his feet and shouted, 'Huzzah!'

Mrs Bradley then burst into speech, telling the company how she had nursed Lady Gwendoline from a babe. The short play began to show alarming signs of running as long as any Haymarket tragedy.

Captain Seaton made a good villain. He had placed a black patch over one eye and leered and cursed with great aplomb. 'You will return with me,' he roared, brandishing the gun. Mr Burridge slipped 'off-stage', ready to fire his own gun harmlessly out of the coffee-room window into the snow to make it sound as if the captain had actually fired his own.

Emily looked at the captain in startled

amazement. Why would no one keep to the script? Instead of pointing the gun at herself and her 'mother', he was pointing it straight at Mr Fletcher.

'I will kill you all,' he snarled. Hannah was also watching. In a flash, as Captain Seaton pressed the trigger, Hannah seized a heavy pewter tray and held it up in front of Mr Fletcher. There was a deafening report and Hannah's hands jerked as a bullet struck the tray and ricocheted off it to bury itself harmlessly in a beam in the ceiling of the coffee room.

Lord Harley snatched the gun from Captain Seaton and muttered, 'Get to your room. I shall speak to you shortly.'

'But I didn't know,' blustered the captain. 'Someone's playing a sore trick on me.'

'Go!' ordered Lord Harley, and Captain Seaton went. Lord Harley said to Hannah, 'Are you all right?'

Hannah nodded, her eyes dancing. 'Another adventure,' she hissed. 'Go on with the play.'

The others seemed so stage-struck, so determined to play their parts, that Hannah was sure very few of them had noticed the shooting. Mr Fletcher made his speech about the forged will. Lizzie curtsied and thanked him most affectingly, and then Mr Fletcher startled everyone by stepping out of his role and clasping Lizzie to his bosom. They stood like that, gazing into each other's eyes, until

Hannah coughed loudly and the couple broke apart.

Lizzie turned to Brave Jack. 'And to you, sir,' she said, leading Emily forward, 'I give my daughter.'

Lord Harley smiled down into Emily's suddenly frightened eyes. 'Forgot it was me, didn't you?' he whispered. He took her in his arms and kissed her, quick and hard, on the lips. The cast applauded themselves, and the landlord and his wife applauded the cast. Emily was shaken. That kiss had burnt, had branded, had caused an upheaval of her senses. Then she recollected that shot. She clutched Lord Harley's sleeve. 'What are we to do about Captain Seaton? He tried to murder poor Mr Fletcher.'

'Keep your voice down,' he whispered fiercely. 'We do not want to alarm the others. Miss Pym knows, but she is keeping quiet.'

Lord Harley went quickly up the stairs to where the captain was sitting sulkily on his unmade bed.

'Well, Seaton?' demanded Lord Harley, 'What have you to say for yourself?'

'I do not know what happened, my lord,' said the captain truculently, 'and that's the truth. I practised with that gun before dinner and Mr Burridge agreed to fire his own out of the coffee-room window. My gun was not loaded, I swear.'

Lord Harley looked at him with loathing.

'You have brought this on yourself. You will leave Mrs Bisley and Mr Fletcher alone, do you hear? If you so much as approach either one of them again, I will shoot you myself.'

Captain Seaton got to his feet, his fists swinging. 'And I am going to teach you a lesson, me fine buck.'

He lunged at Lord Harley, who dodged the blow and then struck Captain Seaton a smashing punch on the chin with his full weight behind it. The captain fell backwards on the bed.

'I will say it once more,' said Lord Harley. 'Do not go near either Fletcher or Mrs Bisley again, or it will be the worse for you.' And, nursing his bruised knuckles, he made his way downstairs.

He found Hannah in the kitchen. The rest were still in the coffee room celebrating the success of the play.

'Did you talk to the captain?' asked Hannah.

'Yes,' he said, rubbing his knuckles. 'What a nasty fool that man is. How could he hope to get away with it?'

'It might have been hard to prove murder,' said Hannah. 'All he had to do was swear he did not know the gun was primed.'

'We must keep a close watch on the captain. What are you doing now?'

'I am preparing a cold collation for supper.'

'You appear to have been deserted by your

123

helpers.'

'Leave them for the moment,' said Hannah. 'I think, however, that we should keep them busy with amusements. If all they are going to do is sit around the coffee-room fire and drink, quarrels are bound to arise. Satan will always find mischief for idle hands.'

'Then let us confound Satan. What do you suggest?'

Hannah wrinkled her brow and pulled her nose. 'Charades might cause more ructions. I have it! Hunt the slipper.'

'I do not see how anyone can try to murder anyone playing that,' said Lord Harley with a grin.

He retreated to the coffee room, where his suggestion was greeted with cries of delight. 'What will be the prize?' asked Old Tom, the coachman.

'No household duties tomorrow,' said Lord Harley promptly.

'The only one who cannot play,' pointed out Emily, 'is the one that hides the slipper.'

'Then let me do it,' offered the landlord. 'I can hide it somewheres where I swear none of you will find it.'

Only Captain Seaton, who had rejoined the group, grumbled it was all tomfoolery.

It was decided to use one of the ladies' slippers, so Lizzie ran upstairs and came back with a pretty red-leather beaded slipper, and handed it to the landlord. He told them to give him half an hour and disappeared.

Captain Seaton sidled up to Lizzie when Lord Harley's back was turned to him. 'You've been avoiding me,' he said. 'You know you are promised to me and a lady never breaks a promise.'

The laughter died out of Lizzie's face. 'We will discuss it some other time,' she said hurriedly and moved away to talk to Mr Hendry, the shabby gentleman who had been one of the two outside passengers.

Emily noticed that even Mr Hendry had a tender look on his face as he talked to Lizzie. He was well enough in his way, she thought, plain and honest-looking and simply dressed and younger than Mr Fletcher, but Emily had set her mind on making a match of it for Lizzie and Mr Fletcher.

The captain waited until they were all busy talking to whisper to Mr Fletcher, 'You just watch it, you popinjay. Mrs Bisley is going to marry me and so she says, so stop sniffing around her, you churl.'

'Odd's fish!' cried Mr Fletcher, enraged. 'Cannot you see the lady would like to have none of you?'

'What's going on there?' demanded Lord Harley sharply, and the captain moved away from Mr Fletcher.

The landlord eventually reappeared, rubbing his hands. 'You'll never find it,' he said. 'Reckon Miss Pym'll have all her helpers on the morrow.'

They all rushed off to search the rooms. Only Lizzie hesitated. She would have liked to play the game with Mr Fletcher, but felt that by doing so she might be putting Mr Fletcher's life at risk. The captain had looked so menacing when he had been talking to him. She went off with the delighted Mr Hendry. Emily had somehow expected Lord Harley to pair off with her, but he had gone off with the coachman. She started to search in a half-hearted way and then with more enthusiasm. It was such a small slipper, it could be anywhere. She even took down pint-sized pewter mugs from their hooks in the taproom and looked inside. It was hard work searching. There were so many nooks and crannies in the inn. Then she decided to try her own bedchamber. She turned everything over and looked under the bed and under the blankets, but there was no sign of the slipper. She was very tired. Bursts of laughter from various parts of the inn showed the others were showing no signs of flagging. Emily decided to lie down for just a little. Ten minutes' rest was all she needed. She lay down on the top of the covers. Her eyes closed almost immediately, and soon she was fast asleep.

Hannah came in a quarter of an hour later and stood in the doorway, looking at the sleeping Emily. She looked very beautiful and innocent in sleep, thought Hannah. Hannah still nursed hopes of a match between Lord Harley and Emily. She turned quickly and went downstairs and searched about, not for the slipper, but for Lord Harley. She found him in the dining-room, looking in a jug on top of the china cupboard.

'My lord,' said Hannah. 'I cannot leave the kitchen for long, for I have some cakes and bread in the oven. Would you be so good as to fetch me my reticule from the Blue Room? It is lying on the armchair by the fireplace.'

'Certainly, ma'am,' he said, looking at her thoughtfully. He wondered what she was about. Miss Pym, he knew, was still servant enough to fetch her own reticule. Still, he made his way up to the Blue Room and then stood, as Hannah had recently done, surveying the sleeping Emily.

So that was it. He grinned. There was no more determined matchmaker than a spinster. He would not play her game, although young Miss Freemantle looked very beautiful and appealing. He walked to the armchair and picked up Hannah's reticule.

She sighed a little and smiled in her sleep. He went to the bed and looked down at her. Her bosom was rising and falling gently. Her skin was very fair, and dark lashes with auburn tips were fanned out on her cheeks.

On a sudden impulse, he sat down on the edge of the bed, leaned down, and kissed her gently on the lips.

127

Emily was dreaming that Lord Ranger Harley was kissing her. She moved her body sinuously in her sleep and wound her arms around his neck. Startled, Lord Harley kissed her more deeply, pressing his hard lips into her soft beguiling pink ones, feeling her small hands caressing the nape of his neck under his long black hair.

Then her body went rigid and her eyes flew open. He immediately released her. She sat up with her face flaming and dealt him a resounding slap across the cheek.

'How *dare* you!' hissed Emily, her eyes blazing.

'If you were not enjoying my kiss,' he said furiously, 'why did you wind your arms around my neck and kiss me back?'

'I was dreaming,' said Emily. 'I was dreaming of Mr Williams.'

'If you are in the habit of kissing him like that,' said Lord Harley, suddenly as furious as she, 'then I suggest you marry him as soon as possible.'

He turned and strode from the room, carrying Hannah's reticule. He went straight down to the kitchen. Hannah was bent over the fire, stirring something in a pot.

'Miss Pym,' said Lord Harley, handing her the reticule, 'do not try to arrange a match for me with Miss Freemantle.'

'I?' exclaimed Hannah.

'Yes, you. She made an enchanting picture,

128

lying there like that, as you very well knew. I am not going to marry Miss Freemantle. She is a silly little girl of no attraction whatsoever.'

'Then,' said Miss Hannah Pym tartly, 'I do not know why you are becoming so exercised. The very sight of her must have filled you with loathing.'

'Pah!' said Lord Harley and went out of the kitchen and slammed the door behind him.

Up in the Red Room, Lizzie was saying to Mr Hendry, 'I am so very tired. I do not think I can search anymore.'

'You are too frail a lady to have to work like a servant in this inn,' said Mr Hendry. 'I would that I could protect you from all ills.'

He had odd light-grey eyes that were suddenly intense. Lizzie realized she was standing with her back to the bed and that he was advancing upon her. 'Why, Mrs Bradley,' she called, suddenly seeing that fat figure in the passage. 'Come and join us in the search.'

'Reckon it won't do much good, m'dear,' said Mrs Bradley, but looking curiously from Lizzie to Mr Hendry. 'Landlord says as how he'll only give us the one hint. It's hanging, he says, where leather hangs.'

'The tack-room?' suggested Mr Hendry.

Now the landlord had said firmly that the slipper was in the inn, but Mrs Bradley said, 'There's a good idea, Mr Hendry. Why don't you go across to the stables and have a look and Mrs Bisley and I will take a rest.'

129

Mr Hendry went with obvious reluctance.

'I don't know if it's the money you got or that dainty way of yours, Mrs Bisley, but the men are around you like flies around the jam pot,' said Mrs Bradley. 'You should be more like our Miss Emily. She got a good hard streak. Pretty as a picture, but not the type of lady to drive the men romantical.'

Emily had been about to enter the room for she had heard their voices, but as she heard the full import of Mrs Bradley's country logic, she shrank back. Her lips trembled. How she longed to be home again with dear Mama and Papa and dear Miss Cudlipp. How she longed to be fussed over and petted.

As she moved away, she heard Mrs Bradley say, 'As to this here slipper, landlord says it's hanging where leather should hang. Where might that be, do you reckon?'

Emily went on down the stairs, turning the problem of the slipper over in her mind to stop her from thinking about anything else. She went into the kitchen and sat down at the table. 'What are you doing?' she asked Hannah.

'I've made some broth from a bit of scrag end hanging in the larder. Thank goodness, the larder is well stocked with meat. I shall prepare a bowl of it for you to take through to Mrs Silvers.'

'I resent waiting on that lady,' said Emily haughtily. 'She looks perfectly well to me.'

'And to me,' agreed Hannah.

'Then why. . . ?'

'Because I doubt if she usually gets one day's rest from one year's end to the other,' said Hannah. 'So humour her.'

Emily suddenly jumped to her feet. 'Leather!' she exclaimed. 'Hanging where leather should be!'

She ran through to the larder and looked up into the darkness of the ceiling where joints of meat hung on hooks. She ran back to the kitchen and seized a chair and carried it into the larder and stood on it. And there, high up among the joints, Lizzie's slipper was hanging.

Emily took a hooked pole and lifted it down, crowing with delight. Hannah came in. 'I've found it!' said Emily. 'No work for me tomorrow. I shall spend the whole day in bed. If I only had a novel to read.'

'Well, go and tell the others it has been found and then come back and get the soup for Mrs Silvers,' said Hannah.

Emily's loud announcement that she had found the slipper received a lukewarm reception, the others having become thoroughly tired of looking for it.

She returned to the kitchen and picked up the tray that Hannah had prepared and took it into Mrs Silvers. 'Just set it down on the table beside the bed,' said Mrs Silvers faintly. Emily did as she was bid and then her eyes fell on a

131

small pile of books on the window-seat. 'Books,' she cried in delight. 'Are there any novels among them?'

'I think so,' said Mrs Silvers. 'Guests leave books from time to time.'

Carrying a candle over to the window-ledge, Emily eagerly studied the titles and then sighed with pleasure. There was a three-volume novel entitled *The Castle of Doom*. She looked inside the volume. The steel engravings were about the most lurid she had ever seen. 'May I borrow these?' she asked.

'Of course,' said Mrs Silvers, now sitting up in bed and slurping soup.

Clasping the precious books to her bosom, Emily left the room and ran up the stairs. Half-way on the stairs, she met Lord Harley, who was coming down. She glanced at him and then the full memory of that sensuous dream sent a tide of hot embarrassment flooding through her body. She gave an odd ducking motion of her head, darted past him, and on up to her room.

Lord Harley tried to put her out of his mind. He should never have contemplated marrying one so young in the first place. In the coffee room, the coachman and the guard were once more at loggerheads. They were drinking dog's nose, a wicked drink consisting of beer laced with gin, damned in London as a 'whore's drink', even in the Coal Hole Inn in the Strand, which was famous for the concoction. The coachman and the guard tried to fight each other, but both were so very drunk that all they managed to do was swipe the air in the general direction of each other. Resisting a temptation to knock their heads together, Lord Harley went out into the storm and across to the stables to see that the horses were being cared for. They were only coaching horses and had nothing to do with him, and yet it was part of his upbringing to see that the horses were warm and well fed before going to bed.

Lizzie and Mr Fletcher had retreated to a cold corner of the taproom, away from the fighting in the coffee room. 'You must be very careful,' said Lizzie quietly. 'Captain Seaton tried to kill you.'

'Are you sure?'

'Yes, very sure. Miss Pym seized that tray and the bullet hit it instead of you. I wish this storm would end so that we could get away and be safe.'

He took her cold hands in his. Hannah Pym peered round the door. She saw them sitting holding hands and shut the taproom door quietly and then stood with her back against it. Things were progressing nicely and she did not want anyone to go in and spoil the budding romance.

'When you say you wish we could get away,' said Mr Fletcher in a voice that trembled slightly, 'I could find it in my heart to wish you meant you and me. . . together.'

Lizzie blushed and hung her head. 'I cannot press my suit,' said Mr Fletcher, 'for I have only a very little money and everyone would say I was pursuing you for yours.'

'No one who knows you could think that,' said Lizzie shyly. He tightened his grip on her hands.

'Oh, my poor heart,' said Mr Fletcher desperately. 'I do so awfully want to kiss you.'

'Then kiss her, you fool!' muttered Hannah, who was listening outside the door. She saw Mr Hendry approaching and held up her hand. 'You cannot go in there, Mr Hendry. I have just washed the floor.'

'But I thought I saw Mrs Bisley go in there with Mr Fletcher.'

'No, you are mistaken,' said Hannah, a militant gleam in her eye.

Inside the taproom, Mr Fletcher closed his eyes and leaned towards Lizzie. His first kiss fell on the side of her mouth, his second on her nose, until, with a shy little laugh, she put her hands on either side of his face and guided his lips to her own.

As soon as Mr Hendry had retreated, Hannah pressed her ear to the door panels. Silence. Beautiful silence, thought Hannah with satisfaction.

7

Werther had a love for Charlotte
Such as words could never utter;
Would you know how he first met her?
She was cutting bread and butter.
William Makepeace Thackeray

Hannah arose promptly at five. The first thing she became aware of was the utter silence. Then she realized what it was. The wind had ceased to blow. She drew back the curtains and opened the window and looked out. It was a clear, starry, frosty morning. But the fallen snow lay deep and high and hard and glittering. They would not be able to travel that day.

She turned and looked at Emily. The girl was lying asleep with a volume of the romance she had been reading lying open on her chest. Hannah gently removed the book. She firmly believed that reading novels was a very bad thing for a young impressionable girl to do. It gave her exaggerated ideas of romance. Hannah shook her head sadly, thinking of Mrs Clarence. All that love and passion that had fizzled away like a guttering candle, leaving two people bound by the ties of marriage who had nothing in common. It was much better, thought Hannah as she went to the kitchen, to find someone one liked and then, if one was lucky, love might follow.

She could see that wretched under-butler in her mind's eye. His name had been Mirabel Flannagan. Mirabel had been a popular name among the aristocracy about fifty years before and, like all fashionable names, had died out at the top level and lingered on at the bottom. Men should have names like George, or John, or Harry, thought Hannah. It was Mirabel's legs that had seduced her mind, Hannah remembered ruefully. He had splendid calves. Also it had been spring when he had begun to pay her attention, and spring was a dangerous time. Now Emily would be a perfectly suitable bride for Lord Harley. She was beautiful and had good bones, so her beauty would last. She was young and would change and grow as soon as she was removed from the doting affection of her parents and governess.

Whether Lord Harley might make Emily a suitable bridegroom did not enter Hannah's head. He was not like the captain, he seemed reasonably kind, he was rich and handsome and a lord. Hannah was very much a woman of her age. Outside the servant class, the only career open to a woman was marriage. As a servant, you were lucky to get a job and asked only that your employer be tolerable. It was the same with marriage. It was just as well, thought Hannah with a little sigh, that everyone knew that life was merely a painful journey to future happiness. But what, nagged a treacherous little voice in her head, if there were no afterlife? What if Heaven had been thought up by the human race because people could not bear the idea that life, which was for most of them wearisome, and which ended in the indignities and pains of old age, was all there was?

She immediately banished the thought, looking nervously around, as if she expected some angel of judgement to fly into the kitchen and take the ungrateful Hannah's legacy away.

The kitchen door opened and Emily walked in. 'What got you out of bed so early?' exclaimed Hannah.

'I felt I should help,' replied Emily primly, although the fact was that the lurid story she had been reading had given her nightmares, and when she had awoken in the dark room she had seen monsters lurking in every shadow.

'I've made some tea,' said Hannah. 'Have a dish of bohea and then you may begin, although you're supposed to be let off work for finding that slipper.'

She put a cup of tea down on the kitchen table. Emily sat down and picked it up and looked at Hannah over the rim. 'Do you really think,' ventured Emily, 'that Lord Harley has no interest in me whatsoever?'

'Not a whit,' said Hannah cheerfully,

kneeling down and stirring up the coals with great vigour.

'Then what, think you, is he looking for in a bride?'

'That's the trouble with men,' said Hannah. 'They don't think. One day, a man decides he wants children and so he enters into the matter like a business deal. That is if he is an aristocrat. He settles on some suitable female and then his lawyers settle the rest.'

'So love does not exist?'

'I think it does,' said Hannah, pulling her nose. 'But it's usually a sham and a deceit and it don't last. Hard on the lower orders because they've got to see the husband day in and day out, but for a young lady like yourself, well, the gentlemen spend most of the time in their clubs, or in Parliament or on the hunting field. Being a married woman would give you a lot of freedom. Settle for someone kind and complacent.'

'How dull,' said Emily, burying her nose in her cup. 'So Lord Harley is not likely to fall in love?'

'He's probably been in love a score of times already,' retorted Hannah cynically.

'So why didn't he marry one of them?'

'Probably weren't marriageable.'

'Does it not seem odd to you, Miss Pym, that such as I must walk to the altar unsullied, and yet a man like Lord Harley can have scores of affairs without losing one whit of his reputation?'

'It's the way the Good Lord has arranged things.' Hannah banged pots and pans with unnecessary noise because she thought there was a lot of truth in what Emily had said, but felt at the same time that a young lady should not even allow such thoughts to enter her head. Furthermore, she was determined not to encourage Emily to think Lord Harley might become interested her in any way. If Emily thought that, her wounded vanity might be satisfied. If she stayed puzzled and hurt by his apparent indifference to her, then perhaps, thought Hannah, she might make more of an effort to engage his attentions.

There came a stamping and shuffling from the yard and then the outside door, which led through the scullery to the kitchen, opened and three shivering maids came in.

'Go tell Mrs Silvers some of her staff have returned,' said Hannah to Emily.

Emily went through to Mrs Silvers' room. As she opened the door, Mrs Silvers sank lower beneath the bed-clothes and demanded feebly, 'Yes, what is it?'

'Some of your maids have managed to return to the inn,' said Emily.

'Then I must rise and see to the lazy-bones,' said Mrs Silvers.

'Are you sure you are well enough?' asked Emily maliciously.

'I be proper poorly, but it be right bad for

them girls to see gentlefolk in the kitchen,' said Mrs Silvers. 'They'll be getting ideas above their stations, and that do lead to laziness.'

Emily returned to tell Hannah that Mrs Silvers was getting out of bed. The kitchen now seemed full of inn servants. It looked as if they had all returned.

'Come along,' said Hannah to Emily. 'We can be ladies of leisure again.'

Emily found she was feeling disappointed. She wondered what she would normally have done with the time had the servants been there all along. Well, she would have read books or checked her clothes for holes and darned any stockings that needed darning and perhaps she would have read novels. How tedious it all seemed now.

Breakfast was served in the dining-room. The coachman had been out earlier and said gloomily that there was no hope of them getting on the road that day. The drifts were piled high and frozen hard.

After breakfast, Hannah suggested it would do them all good to walk for a little into the town. The servants had managed to walk to the inn, so there must be paths through the snow.

Only Mrs Bradley said she would stay by the fire and keep warm.

Emily was tired of her wool gown but did not want to venture out in muslin, even with a fur-lined cloak. She spent longer than usual brushing her hair and buffing her nails and putting on perfume, so that when she went downstairs again, the rest were already impatiently awaiting her at the inn door.

Lord Harley offered her his arm and she took it, glancing up at him in surprise.

'Well, Mrs Bisley,' came Captain Seaton's heavy voice from behind them. 'Are we set?'

He held out his arm. Lizzie shrank back a little. Mr Fletcher firmly drew the widow's arm through his own.

'Why, you . . .' began the captain. Lord Harley swung around and the captain muttered something and fell back.

The sun was shining and snow glittered everywhere. 'How beautiful it is!' cried Emily. Her cheeks were flushed and her eyes were sparkling.

'Yes, very beautiful,' said Lord Harley, looking down at her face.

Emily was conscious of the pressure of his arm. She became quite breathless and then felt a flow of feeling from her own arm to his. She tried to stop it. She began to wish he would release her so that she could breathe properly again.

'Look, there is a baker's shop open,' she cried and disengaged herself from him and ran forward.

'You cannot want to eat again so soon,' protested Hannah. 'You have just had

141

breakfast.'

Emily stayed gazing raptly into the baker's window until she heard them moving on. She then turned around, but found Lord Harley politely waiting for her.

'I do not want to appear rude, my lord,' said Emily, 'but I would rather not take your arm. You see, you are so very tall, I have to reach up, and. . . and. . . it is so awkward . . . and . . .'

He simply smiled in an enigmatic way and waited until she fell into step beside him. Then Emily discovered that the soles of her half-boots, always buffed and polished by the boot-boy at home, had hardly any grip on the rutted icy surface of the winding path between high drifts that led down the main street. She slipped and stumbled and then she had Lord Harley's arm around her waist. The tumult of emotions that contact caused in her body almost made her gasp aloud. It was so dismal to have such a treacherous aching, yearning body when *he* probably felt nothing at all.

Lord Harley was thinking, if this is the effect she has on me when I simply hold her lightly at the waist, what would it be like if I kissed her now? I have kissed her before, but I would like to find out what it would be like if she kissed me back willingly. The more sensible side of his mind chided him for his folly. He was too old and experienced to ally himself to nothing more than a pretty face.

He fairly rushed her along until they caught

up with the others, who were standing admiring giant icicles hanging from a roof. As they moved on again, Lord Harley neatly moved alongside Hannah. Mr Fletcher turned to take Lizzie's arm again but found to his chagrin that Mr Hendry had been there before him. He offered his arm to Emily and both of them walked along in a disappointed silence.

After some time, Hannah suggested they turn back. The sun had gone in and the sky was turning grey again.

As they entered the inn courtyard, Emily, smarting at the way Lord Harley was ignoring her completely, dropped Mr Fletcher's arm and bent down and scooped up a handful of snow.

'What are you doing?' asked Mr Fletcher.

'Watch!' said Emily gleefully.

Lord Harley was nearly at the door of the inn. Emily made a snowball and threw it with all her force.

It caught him on the back of the neck. He swung about and saw Emily laughing at him.

'Minx,' he said, beginning to laugh himself. He made a snowball and flung it back at her.

'Haven't done this since I was in petticoats,' said the coachman gleefully. He made a snowball and threw it at the guard.

Soon they were all indulging in a snow fight, shouting and laughing like children. Everyone was throwing snowballs. Hannah

143

Pym threw snowballs overarm like a cricket bowler and Lizzie was shying the smallest snowballs anyone had ever seen.

And then Mr Fletcher let out a cry and put his hand to his head and collapsed on the snow, blood streaming down his face. Lizzie screamed and ran to him.

Lord Harley pushed her gently aside and loosened the lawyer's neckcloth and felt his pulse. He then looked on the ground near where Mr Fletcher had fallen. There was a large snowball with a piece of something sticking out of it. Lord Harley examined it carefully and then his face grew grim.

'I told you, you churl,' he said, staring at the captain, 'what I would do to you if you did not leave Mr Fletcher alone.'

'What are you talking about?' roared the captain. 'I didn't go near him.'

'You didn't need to,' said Lord Harley. 'You put a large jagged stone inside a snowball and threw it at him.'

'That's a damned lie!' yelled the captain. 'You're persecuting me. You all hate me.'

And to everyone's consternation, he sat down in the snow and began to cry.

'Help me in with Mr Fletcher,' commanded Lord Harley in tones of disgust. Mr Burridge and Lord Harley carried the slight body of the lawyer between them. Lizzie followed them up the stairs and insisted on staying with Mr Fletcher until a doctor could be found.

Hannah entered the bedroom quietly half an hour later. Mr Fletcher had recovered consciousness. Lizzie was sitting beside the bed, holding his hand.

'I would like to ask the pair of you if you plan to wed,' said Hannah.

Mr Fletcher made a feeble noise of protest, for he still had fears of looking like a fortune hunter, but Lizzie said defiantly, 'Yes.'

'I wish you both all happiness,' said Hannah, 'but I beg you, Mrs Bisley, to make an announcement of your engagement at dinner. Once Captain Seaton realizes all hope has gone, then he will trouble Mr Fletcher no further.'

'I will do it,' said Lizzie firmly. 'Where is the captain now?'

'Down below with Lord Harley, still protesting his innocence. Did you notice that great bruise on his chin this morning?'

'Yes,' said Lizzie. 'I wonder what happened?'

Hannah was about to say she was sure Lord Harley had punched the captain, but then decided against it. Lizzie was too tender-hearted and might rush to the captain's side and ruin everything.

'I think he fell over when he was drunk,' lied Hannah. 'Don't forget to make that announcement at dinner.'

The doctor arrived just after she had left and advised Mr Fletcher to stay in bed, after bandaging his head.

The rest of the party assembled around the dinner-table. Lizzie got to her feet and, in a trembling voice and without looking at Captain Seaton, announced her engagement to Mr Fletcher. No one knew what to say, for it was hard to offer hearty felicitations when the rejected lover was seated at the table. Mrs Bradley pressed Lizzie's hand and said, 'Well done, m'dear,' and everyone else murmured some sort of congratulations, except the captain, who glowered into his wine. It began as a silent meal, for everyone was thinking about Captain Seaton at the same time as they tried to pretend he wasn't there. The captain was indulging in what appeared to be a massive fit of the sulks. Emily found herself wishing the staff had not turned up, so that they could all be back in the friendlier atmosphere of the kitchen.

But the coachman, Old Tom, could not bear a silence for long. 'You ladies and gents may think this here storm is a great occurrence, but us coachees is used to disaster and adventure. Yus. Why, I mind when I had a fight on me hands. I'll tell you how it happened. 'Twas when I was driving the Exeter Defiance, the coach what belonged to Mrs Anne Nelson. That lady owned several of the Flying Machines, but it was me what took the Defiance on the Exeter run. Well, as you know, them toll-keepers is supposed to pay

146

over the tolls they collect every Monday morning. But this here toll-keeper at Ilchester was a gambler, and so he had been using the money to play dice. So the trustees told their clerks to serve notice to the guards o' the coaches not to pay the toll-keeper any money. Now that there toll-keeper, he was desperate for the money, and so to make sure he got it, he closed the toll-gates afore the coach arrived. As we was coming up to Ilchester toll, Jim Feathers here, he blew on the yard o' tin, but them gates stayed tight shut. Well, what was we to do? Coach had to get through. So we paid this robber the three shillings. But he was in league with the other toll-keeper further on, so he got a pony and trap and rode ahead o' us and told that there toll-keeper to bar the gates there.

'I wasn't having none o' that. Enough's enough. I got me tool-box and climbed down to chisel the bolt off the gate and them two toll-keepers come at me, one o' them swinging a gurt pike. Jim Feathers here, he come up with the gun and smacks the one wi' the pike over the head with the butt and I land me bunch o' fives in the face o' the other. There ain't no stopping the Exeter coach.'

'It is stopped well and truly now,' pointed out Hannah. The coachman paid her no heed.

'I never race my cattle,' he said, 'but there's some can't resist temptation. Now Harry Lyndon was the best coachman in the whole

147

length and breadth o' Engand and he was on the Portsmouth run and famous for being sure and steady. But one day at the Wheatsheaf at Liphook, disaster fell. He'd been a calm man all his life and was getting on in years, but just as he was changing his horses, two coaches passed him, one, the Hero, and the other, the Regulator, and as they passed him, one coachman cocked a snook at him and the other stuck out his tongue. Now Harry had a fresh team of thoroughbreds hitched up and he was determined to show these cheeky young fellers, as he called them, a thing or two. So he sprung 'em. He passed the Regulator as it was going up Rake Hill. Now he had t'other rival in his sights and he sprung them horses more than ever until a poor soldier on the roof was being thrown up and down like a shuttlecock on a battledore. There was a lady inside the coach screaming like a banshee, but Harry could see nothing but his rival and he drew alongside o' him at the top of Sheet Hill.

'Have you ever been to Astley's Amphitheatre? Ever seen them Roman chariot races? Well, it was like that, said Harry. Down a steep hill they raced, neck and neck. At the bottom of it was a post-chaise, and that terrified post-boy only saved his neck by driving into a ditch. Now Harry, he saw a place on the opposite rise where he could safely pass the Hero. Victory was nearly his.

But do you know what that young whippersnapper what was driving the Hero did? He pulled his horses right across the old coachman's leaders' heads and they pulled the coach all the way up a bank.

'Fortunately, no strap or trace or buckle was broken, but Harry couldn't get nearer the Hero but the back boot all the way to the next stage. But that young coachman lost his job, for three of the Hero's horses never came out of the stable again. Old Harry, well, he never raced again.'

'What became of him?' asked Hannah, her odd eyes shining.

'Died in harness, you might say. Up on the box, arter having brought his team safely home to London, and he snuffed it, just like that, with the reins in his hands. Had to wrench his hands open, he had such a grip on them reins. That's how I'd like for to go.'

Conversation became general. Everyone began to talk about how they would like to die. Mrs Bradley said she would like to die in her sleep; Hannah, anywhere at all so long as it was quick; Emily said she would like to be so very old that death could come as a friend; Lord Harley glanced at her in surprise but said he would like to die in the arms of a pretty woman. He had meant to be flirtatious, but Emily, imagining him in the arms of some opera dancer, glared at him. Captain Seaton, who seemed unsnubbable, said he would like to die in battle, and the rest agreed with Emily.

Hannah suggested a game of cards after dinner provided no one gambled. There were protests at that suggestion, but it was at last decided it was better than doing nothing at all, and they moved through to a large round table in the taproom and played cards until the landlord brought in a bowl of punch and suggested they all have a nightcap, 'courtesy of the house'.

'And so he should,' said Captain Seaton, 'considering we have all been working as his servants without pay.'

'All except you,' said Hannah, but the captain was flushed with wine and had forgotten his earlier misery and paid her no heed.

Emily refused the punch. Hannah had made a jug of lemonade, which was all Emily had drunk at dinner and she felt the better for it.

Everyone began to yawn and an early night was proposed.

They all made their way upstairs, with the exception of Lord Harley, who sat clutching his head. He felt very groggy and was sure he had not drunk all that much. He also felt sure he would wake up in the morning feeling like the devil if he did not do something about himself. He went out to the privvy and was very sick indeed. He splashed his face with water from the pump and then made his way upstairs. Mr Fletcher was lying fast asleep.

Lord Harley still felt groggy. He undressed quickly and climbed into bed and was fast asleep almost as soon as his head hit the pillow.

Emily lay awake reading. She had had to help Miss Pym to bed, a Miss Pym who kept staggering and saying in a thick voice that she would never touch hard liquor again.

The lurid romance continued to hold Emily's attention until late into the night. She put down her book, her heart suddenly hammering hard. There were sinister bump-bump-bump sounds coming from the staircase. Emily slowly sat up in bed. This was what came of reading gothic stories. They made even the most ordinary of household sounds seem sinister. She waited, listening. From downstairs came dragging sounds and then a door opened and closed.

She was just picking up her book again when she heard a sound like wheels coming from the inn yard.

Emily climbed down from the high bed and went to the window, which overlooked the inn yard. She drew back the curtains. She looked down and then stifled a scream.

The yard was flooded with bright moonlight. A man was pushing a handcart, and on the handcart lay a body.

Emily flew to the bed and shook Hannah.

151

'Wake up!' she cried. 'Oh, please wake up.' But no matter how hard she shook Hannah, that lady could not be roused.

Scrambling into her clothes and tying the tapes with trembling fingers, Emily wondered what to do. Then she thought that it was all very simple. She would rouse the men.

She ran to the Red Room and hammered on the door. Silence.

She opened the door and went in. The room was in pitch-darkness. She opened the curtains and let the moonlight flood the room and then drew back the hangings on the bed.

Lord Harley was lying there fast asleep, but there was no sign of Mr Fletcher. All at once Emily was sure that the body in that cart had been that of the lawyer and that the figure pushing it had been Captain Seaton.

'Wake up!' she shouted at Lord Harley.

To her relief, he did wake up and stared at her dizzily.

'Get up!' screamed Emily, jumping up and down in an agony of fear and impatience. 'The captain has killed Mr Fletcher and has gone to get rid of the body.'

Lord Harley looked at the empty space in the bed beside him. 'Get the others,' he said to Emily. 'I will join you shortly.'

Emily ran to the room Lizzie shared with Mrs Bradley but could rouse neither of the women. She tried the coachman and the guard with the same lack of success. Back she ran to

152

the Red Room, gasping that there was something up with everyone, for she could not get them to move.

'Drugged,' said Lord Harley bitterly. 'We've all been drugged. It must have been the punch.'

'I didn't have any. Oh, let us go. Perhaps poor Mr Fletcher is not dead but only drugged.'

'Calmly,' said Lord Harley. 'What exactly did you see?'

'I saw a figure of a man wheeling a handcart through the yard and there was a body lying on the cart.'

Lord Harley pulled on his greatcoat and grabbed a lantern. 'Then there will be tracks of wheels in the snow.'

'Wait a bit,' said Emily. 'I am coming with you.'

'No, this is no work for you, young lady. The whole inn cannot be drugged. There must be at least some of the post-boys.'

'Then I shall come with you until you find help,' said Emily stubbornly.

But the inn and the stables proved to be like the palace of the Sleeping Beauty. The captain had done his work well. 'They are so heavily drugged, it's a mercy he did not kill them all,' said Lord Harley.

'Should we not check the captain's room?' ventured Emily. 'It may have been someone else.'

'Don't be silly,' snapped Lord Harley. 'Who else could it be?'

They were standing in the inn yard. 'Go back,' said Lord Harley, 'and wait for me.'

'I am coming with you,' said Emily, 'and you cannot stop me. See! The marks of the wheels in the snow are very clear, and I shall not freeze. The weather has changed.'

And indeed there was a light warm breeze blowing and behind them came a soft thud as snow fell from the inn roof.

Emily found to her relief that the no longer frozen snow made it easier to walk. She hurried along, trying her best to keep up with Lord Harley's long strides. The wheel tracks led them out of town and into the white arctic desert that was Bagshot Heath.

Three miles outside of the town, the tracks disappeared. Lord Harley swore under his breath.

'There!' cried Emily. 'He has gone off the road. The tracks lead across that field.'

Too excited now to worry about possible danger, Emily plunged into the deep snow of the field. 'It must have been hard going,' she panted. 'See where the cart has been pushed against the deep snow.'

'Wait!' commanded Lord Harley suddenly. The bright moonlight shone down over the field. 'I think I see the cart. Get behind me.'

They moved cautiously towards the cart, but when they reached it there was no sign of anyone, dead or alive.

'He carried Mr Fletcher from here,' whispered Emily. 'You can see the tracks in the snow.'

They ploughed on until the shape of a small barn loomed up against the surrounding whiteness. 'I beg of you, Miss Freemantle,' said Lord Harley urgently, 'let me go ahead. If only I had remembered to bring my gun.'

He quietly approached the door of the barn. There was a smaller door let into the great doors, and it was bolted shut. Lord Harley slid the bolts back, opened the door and stepped in, holding up the lantern.

Mr Fletcher was lying on the floor among bales of hay. His wrists and ankles were bound.

Lord Harley set down the lantern on the floor and knelt down beside the lawyer, drew out his penknife and cut the bonds. Trembling, Emily, who had followed him in, came and knelt beside him as he bent his head and put it to Mr Fletcher's chest. 'Is he dead?' she whispered.

'No, thank God, only drugged like the rest. The wine from the table was sent up to him. Look, there is a portmanteau there. I bet it holds poor Mr Fletcher's clothes. The captain could then let everyone believe he had quit the inn, so that there would be no search for him.'

'And he could come and finish him off at his

leisure,' said Emily, as Lord Harley began to chafe the lawyer's wrists and ankles.

'I do not think he planned on the warmer weather. All he needed to do was to leave his victim here, or so he thought, for a night in the freezing cold, and exposure would do the rest. Then he would untie him and, with his portmanteau beside him, it would seem as if our lawyer had taken refuge in the barn. It would be assumed that Mrs Bisley had forced the engagement and that he was fleeing from her. It was she, if you remember, who announced the engagement. The captain could simply say that Mr Fletcher had begged him to take the widow back because he could not bear the idea of marriage. I think I should carry Mr Fletcher as far as the cart and then wheel him back to the inn. Then I shall rouse the parish constable.'

'What puzzles me,' said Emily, 'is that the fellow I saw pushing the cart was quite slight in build, whereas Captain Seaton is heavy and gross.'

'Moonlight can be deceptive. *What was that?*'

'What?'

'Shhhh!'

Emily clutched at Lord Harley and they both froze. A rising wind blew across the snowy fields outside, and far away an owl hooted mournfully.

'Nothing,' said Lord Harley. 'Well, let's get

our lawyer out of here.'

And then the door banged shut.

Emily let out a squeak of fright.

'Only the wind,' said Lord Harley, 'and if you continue to hold me so close, Miss Freemantle, I shall become persuaded that you love me after all.'

Emily disengaged herself quickly. He walked to the door and pushed it.

Nothing happened.

He pushed harder and then heaved at it with his shoulder.

Then he turned and looked at Emily.

'Someone has locked us in.'

Emily ran to him. 'Try again. Perhaps the wind *did* blow it shut.'

He shook his head.

'The deuce. He must have been hanging about and heard our voices.'

'Why do you not break the door down?' asked Emily in a shaky voice.

'Because it is solid English oak.' He walked back and picked up the lantern and looked about.

'Hurry! Hurry!' pleaded Emily. 'He will come back and murder us.'

'Perhaps not. He will be hoping to make our disappearance look like a runaway as well, or I am not mistaken.' He looked up at the ceiling. Far above their heads was a skylight.

'Let me think,' said Lord Harley, half to himself. 'If I piled up bales of hay to a certain safe height, climbed up with you, and you then stood on my shoulders, you could get through to the roof, slide down, and open the door.'

'Oh, I could, could I?' said Emily, momentarily forgetting her fears. 'Let me tell you, my lord, I have no desire to go back to London with two broken legs.'

'The snow is piled around the barn in drifts and is now soft, and in any case, broken legs will mend. Oh, do not turn missish on me now, I beg of you.'

'I am not missish. But you are expecting me to behave like a man.'

'I am expecting you to behave like a woman of courage. I' faith, why did the Fates land me in this pretty mess with you? Miss Pym would not have hesitated for a minute.'

'A pox on Miss Pym,' screamed Emily, feeling this comparison was the last straw. 'Just get me out of here!'

He began to pile up bales of hay, putting a great number at the bottom to form a base. He had stripped off his greatcoat, coat and waistcoat, and was working away steadily in his ruffled cambric shirt, moving athletically and easily.

Slowly the piles of bales rose until he called down, 'Up with you now. Be careful.'

Emily hauled herself up from one bale to the next, rather like a small kitten climbing a staircase, paws first and legs after, until she was at the top and facing him.

158

'Now,' he said softly, 'I shall lift you on to my back. Open the latch of the skylight and then climb out. But put your head out first and look around and make sure he is not lurking anywhere about.'

She looked up at him, her eyes seeming enormous. 'I am afraid,' she whispered.

He caught her to him and put his arms around her. 'We are all afraid at some time or the other, but we go ahead. Up with you. First, climb on to my back.'

He bent over and Emily moved behind him and began to scrabble up on to his back, one part of her mind registering that it was an indelicate and ridiculous state of affairs, particularly when she found she was sitting on the back of his neck and staring down at the little glow of the lantern on the barn floor. It seemed to be a million miles away.

'Get on with it,' said Lord Harley's muffled voice crossly. 'I cannot see a thing with your skirts over my face.'

She pulled her feet up on to his bent back and he steadied them with his hands. 'Stand up in one swift movement,' he commanded 'and hold on to the latch of the skylight for support.'

Emily closed her eyes and sent up a prayer and then stood upright, her hands searching and scrabbling blindly for the catch. Her fingers found it and she hung on tightly.

'Now,' he said quietly, 'open the skylight.'

159

Lord Harley prayed it would not prove to be rusted shut.

Emily lifted the latch and with one hand threw the skylight full open. It fell back on to the roof with a crash as she steadied herself with her other hand against the side of the opening.

'Hold on tightly,' he commanded, 'and move your feet to my shoulders, and I will start to straighten up. Look out and see if you can see anyone about.'

Emily did as she was bid and soon her head was through the skylight opening. She carefully surveyed the empty fields stretching on either side in the moonlight. 'No one,' she said, twisting her head to look down at him. 'But he may be hiding under the eaves where I cannot see him.'

'That is a chance we will have to take,' came Lord Harley's voice.

'You mean that is a chance I will have to take,' said Emily.

'Are you going to stand on my shoulders arguing all night, or are you going to get on with it?'

Restraining an impulse to kick him in the head, Emily grasped either side of the skylight opening and said, 'Ready.'

He seized her ankles and hoisted her up and through she went. She rolled over on the sloping roof and began to slide, slowly at first and then faster, until she flew off the roof and landed headfirst in a snow-drift. Only fear that Captain Seaton might still be lurking about stopped her from screaming with outrage. She burrowed her way out and made her way around to the barn door and slowly pulled back the bolts and opened it. Lord Harley had already climbed down and was putting on his outer clothes. 'Good girl,' he said, looking at the small snowman that was Emily standing in the doorway. 'Soon have you warm and dry.'

He picked up Mr Fletcher in his arms as easily as if the lawyer had been a child and carried him out of the barn. Emily went ahead, following the path they had made until they came to the cart. 'Push the cart for me,' said Lord Harley. 'No point in putting him on it here, the snow is too soft.'

Emily remembered suddenly how, when she was younger, she had lit the nursery fire herself and the exclamations of horror that had produced from her mother. Her darling hands! She must never spoil them with such hard work when there were servants about. She pushed the cart resolutely to the road, where people walking during the day and a few light carts and wagons had already made something of a track. Lord Harley laid Mr Fletcher tenderly on the cart and then began to trundle it along the road.

'I hope he does not die,' said Emily.

'I think our little lawyer is tougher than he looks. Besides, his love for Mrs Bisley will carry him through anything. Keep very close to me and do not leave me when we reach the inn. Our would-be murderer may still be about.'

'Miss Pym would call this an adventure,' said Emily, beginning to shiver with cold from her fall into the snow-drift.

'No doubt,' he said with a laugh. 'I think she is destined to have many adventures. I think she will attract them. Now you, my kitten, will soon be back with your loving parents and this will all seem like a bad dream.'

Emily walked on in silence. She tried to think of her comfortable home and of Miss Cudlipp, but it all seemed so boring. She tried to think of the beautiful Mr Peregrine Williams but was all too conscious of the power and strength and masculinity of the man beside her.

When they reached the inn, he told her to open the doors for him and lifted Mr Fletcher into his arms. 'I want you to come with me until I undress him and get him to bed. I do not want you to go wandering about the inn on your own.'

He followed Emily up the stairs. She opened the door to the Red Room and lit the candles and stirred up the fire, carefully keeping her eyes averted from the bed where Lord Harley was stripping the lawyer and putting him into his night-shirt. At last he said, 'You may look now. All is respectable.'

'Now what?' said Emily.

'Sit by the fire. I will lock you in here for a moment. I will see if that dog Seaton is in his room. He may have returned and be pretending to be asleep.'

He went out and turned the key in the lock. Emily went over to the bed and felt the sleeping Mr Fletcher's brow. It was reassuringly cool and he slept deeply. Then she noticed a letter on his bedside table with 'Mrs Bisley' written on it. She broke open the seal.

My dear Mrs Bisley [*she read*]. I never was a man of courage and am not yet ready for marriage. I have decided to set out on my own now that the storm has broken rather than stay and face you. Be assured at all times of my admiration and respect. Yr. Humble and Obedient Servant, Fletcher.

Emily was standing with the letter in her hand when Lord Harley came back into the room.

'I cannot understand it,' he said. 'Seaton is in his room and drugged dead to the world. I slapped him and shook him, thinking he was feigning, and I even stuck a pin in the fellow. I am afraid Seaton is not our man. What have you there?'

Emily held out the letter to him and he

read it. 'This is most odd. Mark you the correct grammar and neat hand? I doubt if Seaton even knows how to spell.'

'He may have an accomplice.'

'That we shall endeavour to find out. I shall come with you to your room to make sure all is well.'

'I am so very hungry,' said Emily.

'Well, change your wet clothes first. I'll keep this letter. But first, we had better lock Mr Fletcher in safely.'

He went into the Blue Room before Emily but found only Hannah Pym in a drugged sleep. Then he waited outside while Emily changed her clothes.

'I shall have a whole new wardrobe made of wool and flannel when I return to London,' said Emily. She was wearing a lilac muslin gown with a spencer and with a Norfolk shawl draped about her shoulders.

They went down to the kitchen together. Lord Harley took a lantern and went on down to the cellars to look for a bottle of wine. Emily took out a loaf of bread, a slab of butter and some Cheddar cheese.

When he opened the kitchen door, she was standing by the table clumsily slicing bread, her short auburn curls gleaming in the candle-light, her eyelashes lowered. He felt a sudden wrench at his heart. She looked so very young, so very endearing. He thought of all the women he had known and for the first time in

164

his life felt old and slightly soiled. What Miss Emily Freemantle deserved was a fresh young man of her own age.

She looked up at him and then the smile died on her lips as she saw the bleak expression in his eyes. Something in him had retreated from her. She found that she had been hoping their adventure had brought them together, that it had proved she was not a pampered ninny. Her expression grew as bleak as his own.

'So who do you think our would-be murderer is?' asked Emily, accepting the glass of wine he was holding out.

'I think I might hit on a way to find out.'

'And will you call the authorities, the parish constable?'

'Our villain is clever, whoever he is. Were they not all in their rooms? I am sure we finally looked in every room but the captain's because we were so sure it *was* the captain. I think I have a plan, but you are looking tired, my child. Finish your bread and butter and go to bed.'

8

For my part, I travel not to go anywhere, but to go. I travel for travel's sake. The great affair is to move.

Robert Louis Stevenson

It was noon before the drugged inn became fully awake. And then there was uproar.

The landlord was accused of supplying bad drink. The punch was held to blame, for the servants had drunk what was left over, as they usually did.

'And I,' said Hannah Pym firmly to Lord Harley, 'am convinced I was drugged.'

'Which you were,' he said, and drew her aside and told her of the adventures of the night, ending with the glad news that Mr Fletcher was awake and had no recollection whatsoever of what had happened. 'But,' went on Lord Harley, 'if it is not Captain Seaton, then it is one of the others. But how shall we find out? Shall I gather them together and tell them all what happened and watch their faces to see if one of them betrays himself?'

'No, let me think.' Hannah screwed up her face dreadfully. 'You say this villain left a letter which was supposed to be written by Mr Fletcher?'

'Yes.'

'And it was well written?'

'Too well written to come from, say, the hand of our coachman.'

They were standing in the coffee room at the fire. The coachman came in to say that there was a fine drying wind so that, although the snow was melting fast, he was sure the road would be clear enough to take them on the morrow and without worrying about floods.

'I had better find a livery stable,' said Lord Harley, 'and hire a post-chaise to take Miss Freemantle back to London.'

'And you will go with her?'

'Yes, I shall hire a horse and ride alongside.'

He found Hannah was watching him closely and asked sharply, 'Is anything the matter?'

'No, no,' said Hannah quickly. But she had been hoping for some sign that Lord Harley's adventures with Emily had given him an interest in her. 'Leave the matter of finding out the identity of the villain to me, my lord.'

Dinner found the party all restored to health. Lizzie was not present. She had elected to take a meal on a tray in the Red Room with Mr Fletcher. Neither Lizzie nor Mr Fletcher had been told of the adventures of the previous night. Lord Harley did not want to alarm Mr Fletcher and cause any deterioration in his health, and he did not want Lizzie to be frightened either.

The conversation round the table was cheerful. Everyone was looking forward to going on with his or her journey. 'Tired of sleeping with you,' said Mr Burridge with a grin to Mr Hendry. 'What possessed you to put the bolster between us last night?'

'Because,' said Mr Hendry, 'in your sleep you sometimes appear to think I am your wife and one morning I woke up to find your arms about me.'

This produced a roar of laughter. And then Mr Burridge said, 'Anything planned for this last night, Miss Pym? Charades or plays or the like?'

'I have it,' cried Hannah. 'We will have a letter-writing competition.'

'And I will supply the prize,' said Lord Harley quickly.

'I ain't a strong hand at letter-writing,' grumbled the coachman. 'What's the prize?'

'Five guineas,' said Lord Harley.

There was a gasp of surprise.

'Well, for five guineas I'll try anythink,' said the coachman. 'What's this here letter to be about, Miss Pym?'

'You are leaving this inn without paying your shot,' said Hannah, 'but you must make an excuse which will stop the landlord having you arrested at the next stage.'

'Reckon I could try me hand at that,' said Mrs Bradley. 'Five guineas. I need a new pig and I could get silk for a gown. When do we start?'

'Right after dinner,' said Hannah. 'I am sure after your experiences last night, gentleman, you will be glad to join us ladies and forgo your port.'

Soon they were all gathered around the table in the taproom. Sheets of paper and quill-pens were handed out all round and a large inkwell was placed in the centre of the table.

Emily, who was suddenly aware of the reason for the letter-writing competition, looked at them all eagerly. Which one of them would produce the same handwriting as that on the letter supposed to have been left by Mr Fletcher?

She herself scribbled a short note complaining about dirty towels, barely caring what she wrote. She finished before the others and sat waiting. Then a thought struck her. All the guilty party had to do was to disguise his handwriting. Her heart beat fast. She muttered an excuse and left the taproom. She ran from bedroom to bedroom, looking for something with the handwriting of the occupants. Captain Seaton's room was out, as was the Red Room. She searched the room occupied by the coachman and guard and then the room shared by Mr Burridge and Mr Hendry.

Downstairs, Hannah collected the letters and she and Lord Harley retired to a corner to study them.

'Nothing like,' said Hannah gloomily, surreptitiously comparing the letter from Mr Fletcher's room with the others.

'And I was so sure your plan would work that I sent the landlord to fetch the constable,' said Lord Harley.

Then Emily quietly came into the room and handed Hannah a torn scrap of paper with writing on it and in a whisper told her where she had found it.

'Come along there!' called the coachman. 'Who's won?'

'While Lord Harley makes up his mind,' said Hannah, 'I would like to tell you a story.'

'Oh, I'd like that,' said Mrs Bradley cheerfully. 'Nothing like a good tale to while away a winter's night.'

'Once upon a time,' said Hannah, 'there was a pretty widow who had run off on the stage-coach with a military gentleman who was anxious to marry her and get her money before anyone else did.' The guard glanced at the captain and nudged the coachman.

'But on the journey, she met a lawyer, a nice, kind man, and fell in love. The stage-coach party found themselves stranded at an inn. To while away the time, they put on a play. In that play, the military man was supposed to pretend to fire a gun at the ladies, while another passenger fired *his* gun out of the window to make it all seem lifelike. But when the military man fired his gun, it went off, and as he had been pointing it at the lawyer, his rival, he was suspected of attempted murder, for the lawyer would have been most surely killed had not one passenger quickly put a metal tray in front of him to deflect the bullet.'

'I never loaded that gun,' shouted the captain, turning quite purple with outrage. Hannah ignored him and went on.

'After the day of the play, the party decided to take a walk, for the storm had ceased. A young lady in the party started a snowball fight. Someone tried to injure the lawyer by throwing a snowball with a stone in it and everyone blamed the military gentleman.'

'And they were wrong,' growled the captain.

'And they were wrong,' echoed Hannah.

An air of tension crept into the group.

'So our villain hit on another plan. He drugged a bowl of punch, being careful not to take any himself. While everyone was asleep, he went to his own room and pretended to be asleep, and when he was sure his companion was unconscious, he rose and dressed and went to the lawyer's room. He dressed him and then left a note beside the bed supposed to be from the lawyer saying he did not want to marry the widow after all and was leaving. Then he lugged the body of the lawyer downstairs and put it in a handcart and wheeled him far out of town to a barn, where he left him with his hands and feet bound, meaning to release him the next day, when the cold had finished the poor fellow off. He left the lawyer's portmanteau in the barn beside him.

'But someone saw the villain leave the inn—a pretty young maiden who roused a handsome lord, one of the guests, and together they went out and followed the wheel tracks in the snow. As they found the lawyer, the villain locked them in the barn until he could think of a way of dealing with them. But they escaped and brought the lawyer back and set about discovering who this villain might be. And they did and they found out that we have a would-be murderer in our midst.'

There were sharp exclamations of alarm.

'But surely you looked in the rooms,' said Mr Hendry. 'Anyone missing would have proved the identity of the villain.'

'Apparently no one was missing,' said Hannah, 'and that, Mr Hendry, was because you put the bolster on your side of the bed and made it look as if there was someone lying in it.'

'You're mad! You're lying,' cried Mr Hendry.

'Miss Freemantle found a scrap of paper in your luggage, part of a letter you had written, and with your signature, Mr Hendry,' said Hannah sternly. 'We compared it with the letter by Mr Fletcher's bed, and the

172

handwriting matches exactly. You wanted the widow for yourself. No doubt, given time, had your plan succeeded, you would have left evidence to point to Captain Seaton. I think that before the play, it was you that loaded that gun, but why he should so fortuitously point it at Mr Fletcher, I do not know.'

'I know!' shouted the captain, leaping up. 'It was Hendry who told me it would be fun to give him a scare. That's why I pointed the gun at that pip-squeak of a lawyer.'

'Look out!' screamed Mrs Bradley suddenly. 'He's got a gun.'

Mr Hendry backed towards the door, a small gun levelled at the assembly.

Behind him, the door slowly opened. A constable and two watchmen suddenly dashed in and pinioned Mr Hendry's arms to his sides. He was led off struggling and screaming.

He left behind a shocked silence. 'Well done!' said Lord Harley suddenly, smiling at Emily. 'If you had not found that scrap of paper, we would have been hard put to find evidence against him.'

'Shall we all need to stay here until the trial?' asked Emily.

'No,' said Lord Harley. 'I shall take along that piece of paper and the letter as evidence and I will send my lawyer to be present at the trial.'

'Reckon that letter-writing thing was all a hoax,' said Mrs Bradley.

'I'm afraid it was,' said Lord Harley, 'and so I shall give a guinea to you, one to Mr Burridge, one to our coachman, and one to the guard.'

'Don't Miss Freemantle get anything?' asked Mrs Bradley. 'Seeing as how it was her quick wits what trapped the fellow.'

'I think Miss Freemantle will consider a journey home in a comfortable post-chaise reward enough,' said Lord Harley.

They sat up late that night, talking over the attempted murder. Lizzie and Mr Fletcher entered and the whole tale had to be told over again.

'Are you sure it will be safe to travel on tomorrow?' Hannah asked the coachman. 'Despite the good drying wind you described, such a quantity of snow will surely produce floods.'

'We'll get through all right,' said the coachman, who, like most of his breed, was never happier than when seated up on the box. The prolonged inactivity at the inn was beginning to irk him.

'We shall not be going on,' said Lizzie quietly. 'I see no reason to go to Exeter. Mr Fletcher and I will stay here until he has fully recovered his strength and then take the up coach back to London.'

'It's a hard business when a respectable man like me should first be accused of attacking that fellow and then have his promised bride go off with him,' said the captain.

'Mrs Bisley has made her choice,' remarked Lord Harley, 'and I suggest you accept it with good grace.'

'I've never been so shoddily treated,' grumbled the captain. 'And now that the staff are back at the inn, I don't see as how a gentleman like myself should be expected to dine at the same table as a coachman, a guard and an outsider.'

'Now there ain't no call for you to get uppity.' Mrs Bradley looked into her basket as if hoping to find a medicine to cure snobbery. 'Here's his lordship, turned his hand to everything to help, while you sat about doing nothing. I know we don't normally dine with them outsiders, but things is different this time.'

The outsiders, that is, the passengers who travelled on the roof, were always looked down on by the insiders, and landlords had learned never to put them at the same table. Mr Burridge, who was seated next to Captain Seaton, edged his chair away. 'Would never dawn on you that I might be pertickler over which company I keep.'

'It looks as if we shall have the carriage all to ourselves and the captain,' said Hannah to Mrs Bradley. She turned to the coachman. 'Surely you could allow Mr Burridge to travel inside with us until you take up more

175

passengers?'

But here the coachman dug in his heels. The outsider had only paid an outsider's fare, and there was no way he was going to allow Mr Burridge to travel on the inside.

They were all separating already, thought Hannah gloomily. Rank and pecking order were asserting themselves. And what of Emily and Lord Harley? He barely looked at her. Now that the staff were all back, there was no cozy kitchen to which to retreat for private confidences.

Lord Harley rose to his feet. 'I am going to walk to the livery stables to make sure a post-chaise will be ready for the morning.'

'I need a breath of fresh air,' said Hannah quickly, 'I shall accompany you.' She ran to fetch her bonnet and cloak.

But as she walked through the slush to the livery stables, Hannah found Lord Harley rather distant and uncommunicative. Once more she felt like a servant and thought that any probing about his feelings for Emily might be treated as presumption.

After Lord Harley had ordered the post-chaise and they were returning to the inn, Hannah could not bear it any longer and said impulsively, 'I feel Miss Freemantle's parents had the right of it. You would make a very suitable couple.'

'The difference in age and experience is too great,' he said, his voice seeming to come from a great height.

'But—'

'Miss Freemantle does not love me, nor I her. Now let that be an end of the matter, Miss Pym.'

Hannah stroked the expensive material of her cloak, almost as if to reassure herself she was no longer a servant. He turned and faced her at the inn door. 'I am grateful to you, Miss Pym,' he said, 'for all the help you have given, for all the meals you have cooked, and for your bravery and gallantry.'

Hannah looked up at him, bewildered at the sudden compliment. He smiled down at her and then stooped and kissed her lightly on the cheek.

It was a crying shame, thought Hannah, as he held open the inn door for her, that he could not, or would not, marry Emily Freemantle.

'Please tell Miss Freemantle that we leave at six o'clock in the morning,' said Lord Harley.

'Would you not like to tell her yourself?' suggested Hannah, faint but pursuing.

'I see no need for that. Good night, Miss Pym.'

Emily was getting ready for bed when Hannah entered the Blue Room. 'Lord Harley has hired a post-chaise and he will be ready to escort you to London at six o'clock in the morning,' said Hannah.

'Very well,' said Emily in a quiet little voice. 'As you can see, I have already packed. I suppose I had better wear that woollen dress again. I am sick of the sight of it.'

'Never mind,' said Hannah. 'You will soon be back with your parents.'

'Yes.' Emily looked bleak.

Hannah awoke at five o'clock and busied herself getting dressed and then roused Emily. Emily herself dressed very quickly and Hannah noticed the girl did not pay any particular attention to her appearance.

She followed Emily down to the dining-room. There was no sign of Lord Harley. The landlord served Emily with toast and tea and told her that Lord Harley was already outside and waiting.

Feeling very low and sad, Hannah followed Emily out of the inn. Emily stood with one little foot on the step of the post-chaise. Lord Harley, already mounted on a large black mare, was waiting alongside.

'May I have your address in London, Miss Pym?' asked Emily. 'I would like to write to you.'

'Of course. One moment.' Hannah ran back into the inn and came out with a sheet of paper and a lead pencil. She tore the paper in half and wrote her address on one piece and then said, 'And your address, Miss Freemantle?'

As Emily wrote it down, Hannah called up

178

to Lord Harley. 'And where might you be found, my lord?'

She waited anxiously for his reply, half expecting a snub. 'St James's Square,' he said. 'Number twenty-seven.'

Emily handed over her address and climbed into the post-chaise. Hannah waved as the carriage drove off and then turned away sadly, for Emily had had tears in her eyes.

The coachman lumbered out and said he would be hitching up a team and would be obliged if Miss Pym could hurry the others up, as they had just started their breakfast.

But Hannah collected more sheets of paper and pen and ink from the taproom, where they had been left lying from the night before. She went into the Red Room and gently shook Mr Fletcher awake.

'I need your help,' she told the startled lawyer. 'I have letters to write and do not have either the education or the necessary delicacy.'

*   *   *

Mrs Bradley was disappointed in Hannah Pym. The captain had not joined them. He had decided to stay at the inn and wait for the next coach back to London. Mrs Bradley and Hannah were therefore alone inside the coach as far as Salisbury, where they took up more passengers, but Miss Hannah Pym turned out

179

to be a sadly silent companion. Even when they had to drive through a flood and the water came up as far as the windows, Hannah remained silent and morose.

But at Salisbury, Hannah asked the coachman where to find the mail coach, and on learning that it left the Angel, St Clement's, at four, set off at a run. When she returned, Mrs Bradley found that Hannah was once more her talkative self and looking forward to the rest of the journey. On they went through towns and villages— Shaftesbury, Sherborne, Yeovil, Crewkerne and Chard—and each mile they went, the weather got better and the road firmer.

But when the Exeter Fly crossed into Devon and the end of the journey was in sight, Hannah Pym grew nervous and restless again. At one point she said aloud, 'Oh, what have I done? What have I done?'

'Whatever do be plaguing you, m'dear?' asked Mrs Bradley anxiously, but Hannah only shook her head and said mysteriously that she must have been mad.

And Mrs Bradley, who had been going to ask Hannah for her address, decided that she really was mad and changed her mind. For Hannah said she was returning to London by the next up coach and had only travelled to Exeter for 'the experience'.

At the Old London Inn, Hannah sat by the window of the coffee room wondering what had become of Emily Freemantle and whether she would marry her Mr Williams, and whether her experiences at the inn had made any change in her character at all.

*　　*　　*

While Hannah was sitting brooding in Exeter, Emily had just returned from a drive in the Park with Mr Peregrine Williams. She felt restless and bored and suffocated. Her parents had welcomed her back with open arms and crying with remorse. If Mr Williams was what she wanted, then she should have him. Lord Harley had explained the dangers she had endured with such fortitude. To think they had driven her to that! And all the time Emily had a nagging feeling that she would have felt more at ease if they had berated her for her selfishness. She had told Miss Cudlipp all about her adventures, but Miss Cudlipp had exclaimed in horror at everything and could not understand when Emily had tried to explain that some of the experiences had been fun.

Some new caution in her had made her tell her parents that it might be a sensible idea if she got to know Mr Peregrine Williams a little better before making any commitment and they gladly agreed.

And so she had.

But she could find nothing at all beneath

181

the beautiful face to interest her. She was to make her come-out at the Season. She was to have the best of gowns and hats. It seemed as if her parents could not do enough for her, and Emily miserably felt she did not deserve any of it. At times, she thought of Hannah Pym and envied that lady her freedom. She did not think of Lord Ranger Harley. By a tremendous effort of will, she banished him from her mind. To think of him would be too painful. He had made her feel ugly and unwanted, and although her mirror and the doting Miss Cudlipp told her she was beautiful, she could no longer take any pleasure in her appearance.

'Did Mr Freemantle give you your letter?' asked her mother when Emily walked into the drawing-room.

'No, Mama.'

'It is over there, on the console table.'

Emily picked it up and looked at it curiously. There was a heavy red seal on it, but so mangled that she could not make out what it was supposed to represent. The paper was of quite poor quality, so it was probably from Hannah Pym, not Lord Harley. But Hannah was a connection with all those great adventures. Emily opened it and scanned the page eagerly. A blush rose to her cheeks and she read it carefully again, almost unbelievingly.

'Who is it from, dear?' asked her mother.

'Just some lady I met on the journey. I must go up to my room and take off my bonnet.'

Emily fairly ran up the stairs and into her room and locked the door. Then she sat down and looked at that precious letter again. It was not from Hannah. She had only said that until she had time to read and reread the letter. It was from Lord Harley.

Dear Miss Freemantle [*she read*], I felt I must write to you, for I find I lack the courage to call. I think of you constantly, of your charm and beauty. I was held back from declaring my interest because of the difference in our ages. I am thirty-two years old and feel like some elderly satyr in your presence. But love has given me hope. If you care for me a little, could you find it in your heart to meet me alone by the canal at the north end in St James's Park at nine o'clock in the morning on Friday, the 31st of this month? If you cannot, then ignore this letter and be happy with your Mr Williams, but be always assured of my love, respect, and admiration. Harley.

Emily put down the letter. She felt such a glow of happiness and elation that she wanted to shout aloud.

But two whole days to wait. How could she contain herself until then?

Lord Harley at that time had just returned from riding in the Park. He had been blessed by a glimpse of Emily and her cavalier. He thought bitterly that they made a handsome pair and considered himself to have had a lucky escape. He seemed to spend most of his days telling himself how lucky he was to have escaped the clutches of the Freemantle family. He picked up the morning's post, which he had not bothered to read earlier, and carried it into the library. He flicked through it, pausing when he came to a letter written on cheap paper. He opened it first and then sat looking at it in amazement.

Dear Lord Harley [*he read*], I can hardly find the courage to pen this letter to you. I have thought of you often since our adventures at the inn at Bagshot. I wanted to show you the warmth of my feelings towards you then, but was so afraid I had given you a disgust of me by my unruly and selfish behaviour. If you have any feeling for me, can find it in you heart to forgive me, please meet me at the north end of the canal in St James's Park on Friday the 31st of this month at nine o'clock. Yr. Humble and Obedient Servant, E. Freemantle.

A bewilderment of feelings and memories assailed him; Emily's lips against his own,

Emily in the barn, bravely climbing up to the skylight, Emily wilful, Emily humorous, Emily with those huge violet eyes and glowing auburn curls. For a short moment, he felt quite dizzy with elation. Then he read the letter slowly again and that elation fizzled and died. He was all at once sure Emily had not written that letter. He turned it over and studied the frank. Salisbury. And Salisbury was on the road to Exeter and the travelling matchmaker had been on the road to Exeter. He threw the letter away from him and cursed loudly. He would find that crooked-nosed interfering spinster and wring her neck! She had probably sent the same kind of letter to Miss Freemantle and that gullible child would no doubt be waiting in St James's Park on Friday, or would show the letter to her parents and ask them to tell him to leave her alone.

For the next two days, he buried himself in affairs of business, trying to put that trickster's letter out of his mind. But by Friday morning, when he had heard nothing from Miss Freemantle, he realized that she had believed the letter she had no doubt got herself and planned to go to St James's Park and keep that appointment.

The best thing he could do was to go himself and tell her gently that they had been tricked. She would no doubt be relieved.

It was a cold, frosty morning when he set out, driving his curricle. He reined in at the

185

north end of the ice-covered canal, which was lined by rotting lime trees, and stood and waited, looking unseeingly at the red brick front of Buckingham House. Frost sparkled everywhere and it was bitter cold. Then he saw a hack approaching.

The hack stopped and Emily Freemantle climbed down and paid the coachman.

She was wearing her blue cloak and a very fashionable bonnet under which her short curls glowed in the sunlight.

As the hack plodded off she turned towards him, smiled shyly, and held out both her hands.

All his determination to tell her the letters were forgeries fled from his mind. He walked straight up to her and seized her hands and looked down into her face.

She stood there laughing and blushing and looking adorable.

He caught her in his arms and bent his head and kissed her and Emily kissed him back and it was all he had ever dreamt of. Senses reeling and deaf to the conventions and blind to the interested gaze of a park warden, they kissed and kissed with single-minded passion. At last he raised his head and smiled down at her. 'Marry me,' he said. 'Very soon.'

'How soon?' demanded Emily.

'As soon as we can. Let us go and tell your parents our news.'

Mr and Mrs Freemantle both cried with

delight. Miss Cudlipp looked astounded and kept saying feebly, 'But Mr Williams? Poor Mr Williams.'

But she was pulled from the room by Emily's parents. The happy couple must be left alone for ten minutes to exchange their vows.

As soon as the door closed behind them, Lord Harley seized Emily in his arms and kissed her breathless. 'Can you bear to be married to such an old man?' he said at last.

'You are only thirty-two,' said Emily.

'I am more than that, my child. I am thirty-three.'

'But you said in your letter—'

He silenced her with another kiss and then said, 'Do you have that letter with you?'

'Yes, it is here in my reticule.'

'Let me see it.'

Emily took it out and handed it over. He read it and then began to laugh. 'The cunning old trout,' he said.

'Who? Oh, what are you talking about?'

'My love, I never wrote that letter and I knew as soon as I got one supposed to come from you that you had not written it either. If I am not mistaken, both letters were sent by the interfering Miss Hannah Pym.'

'But. . . but. ..' said Emily desperately. 'You came and you said you loved me . . . You were joking!'

'My darling, not I. I bless Miss Pym and all

her interfering ways. Kiss me again!'

Emily looked up at him nervously. In that moment, he looked a stranger, a stranger with thick black hair and black eyes and richly dressed. Then he smiled at her and her heart did a somersault. She wound her arms tightly about him as she had done in her dream and raised her face to his.

Her parents stood nervously outside the door, listening to the long silence from within. At last they opened the door. The couple were so wrapped up in each other that they did not notice them. 'Do something,' hissed Miss Cudlipp tearfully. 'Poor innocent Emily!'

'Go to your room,' said Mr Freemantle savagely. 'Our Emily's growed up!'

9

Love's like the measles—all the worse when it comes late in life.
                    Douglas William Jerrold

Hannah Pym was back in her two small rooms over the bakery in Kensington. She wanted to call on Sir George Clarence and recount her adventures. But how could she enjoy telling her adventures when her conscience was so sore?

She remembered getting poor little Mr

Fletcher to write those letters. She had bullied him into it, although he had protested that it was surely immoral to stoop to forgery. She had eagerly studied the social columns for days now, hoping for an announcement of a wedding between Lord Harley and Miss Freemantle. Such an announcement, she felt, would lift the terrible guilt from her mind. She could then call on Sir George and plan her next expedition.

What adventures she had had! And how miserable that she could not even turn them over in her mind without coming across the great stumbling block of her own bad behaviour.

She chided herself. She had always been nosy, had always interfered in other people's affairs. Never again. When she took her next journey on the Flying Machine, she would look at the scenery and ignore the other passengers.

The two little rooms were very dark and bleak, but she did not want to set about looking for a cottage until she had satisfied her lust for travel and adventure. But adventure to Hannah was not only travel on the stage-coach. It meant adventuring into other people's lives. When there had been a regular staff at Thornton Hall, she had enjoyed herself immensely busying herself in their affairs. She thought of going back to look at Thornton Hall and then rejected the idea.

There would be some strange caretaker and his wife in residence. There would be no one to talk to.

For the first time in her busy life, Hannah began to feel lonely. She put on her cloak and hat and went out into Kensington Village and spent far too much on two bunches of spring flowers, lately arrived from the Channel Islands, to give her drab living quarters some colour.

But once the flowers were arranged in vases, she began to feel cheered.

And then there came a knock at the door. She wondered who it could be. The baker had been paid rent in advance.

She smoothed down her gown and opened the door and then fell back a pace.

Lord Harley and Emily Freemantle stood on the threshold.

The entrance was dim and Hannah's sharp eyes scanned their faces hopefully, but both were looking solemn and severe.

'Come in, Miss Freemantle, my lord,' said Hannah nervously. She raked the fire to a glowing red and put a kettle on it. 'You will take tea?'

'We should be furious with you, Miss Pym,' said Lord Harley, 'and you know why.'

It was no use trying to pretend otherwise. 'How did you know?' asked Hannah miserably.

'Because I would not write such fustian, and

neither would Miss Freemantle.'

Hannah's eyes filled with tears. 'Pray forgive me,' she said. 'You both seemed to be very suited, and I thought . . .'

She gave a pathetic little sob.

'Put her out of her misery,' said Emily with a laugh, and Hannah looked at the girl's glowing face, hope dawning on her own.

'Yes, you travelling matchmaker,' said Lord Harley. 'Your plan worked. We are come to invite you to our wedding.'

'Oh, my lord,' gasped Hannah. 'It is more than I deserve. When is the marriage to take place?'

'In three months' time,' said Emily. 'You will receive an invitation very shortly.'

To Emily's consternation Hannah sat down suddenly and began to cry in earnest. 'I have been feeling so guilty,' said Hannah, mopping her eyes. 'So very guilty. I *forced* poor Mr Fletcher to write those letters for me, and when I went to say goodbye to him at the inn, he could barely bring himself to speak to me.'

'Poor Miss Pym,' said Lord Harley. 'Now what about some tea?'

Hannah busied herself making a pot of tea and then ran down to the baker's to buy cakes. By the time she returned, Lord Harley and Emily were wrapped in each other's arms. She retreated to the passage and coughed loudly and then walked in again.

The couple were once more apart and

Emily began to talk about their adventures at the inn. Lord Harley said that Mr Hendry's background had been discovered. He had been an apothecary's assistant in London and had been trying to court his master's daughter. The apothecary had sent him packing and discovered after Mr Hendry had left that he had stolen money from the shop and a quantity of drugs. 'Will he hang?' asked Hannah uneasily. In an age of mass hangings that were always well attended, it was surprising the number of people who loathed the very idea of that ultimate punishment.

'I do not think so,' said Lord Harley. 'I believe he will be transported.' The couple then began to talk generally of their adventures. Hannah joined in, but after a while Lord Harley and Emily seemed only to want to turn over and over again how they first came to fall in love, and Hannah felt excluded from the glowing circle that seemed to surround the happy pair.

When they left, she found she was feeling more alone than ever. She could never have been in love with that under-butler. For Lord Harley and Emily had been radiant and exalted by love. Hannah could never remember having felt like that.

But a cheerful thought came into her mind. Now she was free to go and see Sir George. First, she sat down and wrote Mr Fletcher a letter. He had given her the address of a friend in London where he had said he would be staying until he married Lizzie. She told him that his forgeries had done the trick. Then she sealed the letter and put on her hat and cloak and took the letter to the post.

Then she looked at Sir George's card, hailed a hack, and gave the driver directions to Green Street in Mayfair.

Only when she had rung the bell and an imposing butler was standing looking at her did Hannah realize two things. Firstly, a lady did not call at a gentleman's town house, and secondly, she did not even have a card to present.

Her cloak and hat were of the finest material, but servants, she knew only too well, had an inbuilt sense of who was Quality and who was not.

'I am come to see Sir George Clarence,' said Hannah. 'I am Miss Pym.'

The butler did not hesitate for a moment.

'Sir George is not at home,' he said and closed the door in Hannah's face.

Sir George was walking into the hall, drawing on his gloves as the door slammed.

'What was that?' he asked.

'A person by the name of Miss Pym. She did not even have a card, sir.'

'Pym?' Sir George looked puzzled for a moment and then his face cleared. 'Oh, Miss *Pym*. And I told her to call.'

The butler sprang to the door and opened

193

it as Sir George hurried out. Sir George looked to right and left and then saw a thin dejected figure just turning the corner of the street. He walked swiftly along and finally caught up with Hannah.

'Miss Pym,' he called.

Hannah turned round and looked at him. She had forgotten how handsome and distinguished he looked with his piercing blue eyes and silver hair.

She tugged at her nose in embarrassment and said croakily, 'I should not have called on you, sir, at your home. I was acting as a servant, you see, and I forgot I did not even have a card to present.'

'And I should have told you to write to me so that we could make an arrangement to meet,' said Sir George. 'I was on my way to my club, but I would rather hear your adventures. It is not far to Gunter's, and it is a fine day.' He held out his arm.

Hannah gingerly took it and then cast little glances to right and left, hoping one of the former servants from Thornton Hall might appear and see her walking so grandly with Sir George Clarence.

Once seated in Gunter's, Hannah began her tale. Sir George leaned back in his chair and studied those odd eyes of the ex-housekeeper. They would glow blue with happiness, flash green with excitement, or turn gold when she was serious. He listened enthralled to her tale of the highwayman, the snowstorm, the incarceration at the inn, and the perfidy of Mr Hendry, and then in increased amusement as she told him how she had cajoled Mr Fletcher into writing those letters.

'Now that was very bad and mischievous of you,' said Sir George gently. 'Perhaps it is just as well Lord Harley does not know your direction, or you might have found yourself in court.'

'But it all came well in the end,' said Hannah happily. 'For this day Lord Harley and Miss Freemantle called to invite me to their wedding.'

He laughed and laughed and then he said, 'So now you have had your fill of adventures, you will be glad to settle down.'

'Oh, no,' said Hannah. 'I have only just begun.'

'And where are you bound next?'

'Bath,' said Hannah. 'I think I shall go to Bath.'

'Are you sure? If it is adventures you crave, I cannot think you will find any on the road to Bath. It is a good easy road and I think the worst of the winter weather is over. And Bath itself! Genteel invalids and filthy tasting water.'

'No, I always wanted to go to Bath. Do you know, sir, that sometimes I dream that on a journey I will meet Mrs Clarence. I know she did a very bad thing, but I remember her with affection. Besides, she will be free to marry now and might not know it.'

'My brother's death was published in all the newspapers,' he said. 'Mrs Clarence has no doubt read one of them or has been told by a friend. Where do you reside at present?'

'I have taken two small rooms above a bakery in Kensington.'

'Cannot you do better for yourself? If I can be of any help . . .'

'You are too kind, sir. But I would like to travel first and then find some place pleasant to live afterwards. But you have heard all my news and I have not once asked you about yourself, sir.'

'I have been busying myself with Thornton Hall. Perhaps I shall sell it. But it is such a bleak, ugly place that I became obsessed with a desire to see how it would look with pretty gardens and some decoration. If you go to Bath, you will see from the road that the gardeners have already begun work.' He began to talk of all the improvements he was making and Hannah studied him covertly, trying to remember every detail: the high-nosed face, the bright blue eyes, the hair that was so white and fine, the splendour of his dress. He was wearing a coat with a high collar and short waist made of plum-coloured silk, nankeen breeches, and gold-and-white-striped stockings. A diamond flashed in the whiteness of his cravat and a diamond-and-sapphire ring sparkled on one of his long white fingers.

Hannah had opened her cloak when she sat down and hoped he noticed her dress of fine glazed cambric, one of Mrs Clarence's gowns. Mrs Clarence had always been almost ahead of the current fashions, and fortunately her gowns were high-waisted, so that Hannah had had to make very little alteration.

She dreaded the moment when he would rise to leave. Her pleasure in his company was tinged with a bitter-sweet flavour. She could never feel entirely at ease with him, always conscious of her lower rank, always feeling out of place, very much like a servant strayed into a world in which she not only did not belong but to which she would never belong. But he seemed in no hurry to take his leave and they talked on amicably until the blue light of dusk began to fill Berkeley Square outside and the lamplighter was up on his long ladder filling the parish lamps with whale-oil and lighting them.

And then a lady came up to their table. Hannah looked up. Sir George rose to his feet and Hannah stopped herself just in time from rising as well.

'Sir George,' carolled the lady. 'I have not seen you this age.'

'Good afternoon, Mrs Courtney,' said Sir George. 'Miss Pym, may I present Mrs Courtney. Mrs Courtney, Miss Pym.'

Mrs Courtney sank down gracefully in an empty chair at their table without being invited. Hannah's heart sank. She remembered Mrs Courtney. She had called two years before to see Mr Clarence, and it had been the general opinion of the servants that the lady, a widow, was husband-hunting. She was extremely elegant with a pretty, faded face. She was wearing a mauve crepe gown trimmed with groups of tucks and with a fold of silk of the same colour inserted in between. On her head was a headdress of intricately folded mauve silk. Her large greenish eyes rested curiously on Hannah, much as they had rested on the housekeeper two years before when she had quizzed Hannah closely about the state of Mr Clarence's mind and whether he intended finally to divorce his errant wife.

Sir George was talking generally about the weather, plays he had seen, and mutual friends. Mrs Courtney raised her quizzing-glass and studied Hannah through it and then let it fall. 'Haven't we met?' she asked, interrupting Sir George.

'I do not think so,' said Hannah. On her own, she would have told the truth, but she did not want to disgrace Sir George by admitting to having been a servant.

'Strange.' Mrs Courtney's green eyes fairly snapped with curiosity. 'And are you an old friend of Sir George?'

'A very old friend,' said Sir George firmly.

198

'We have not seen each other this age, and there is so much to talk about.'

'I am sure you are both wishing me gone,' said Mrs Courtney with an artificial laugh but showing no signs of getting to her feet.

'I could never bring myself to say such a thing.' Sir George leaned back in his chair and smiled blandly on Mrs Courtney. 'But I fear you will find Miss Pym and me boring company, for we have so much to discuss.'

Mrs Courney bridled. The hint was too obvious. She rose to her feet. 'But I am so sure I have met you, Miss Pym. Do not worry. I shall recall where and when. I have an excellent memory.'

'And that is a threat,' said Hannah gloomily when Mrs Courtney had left the shop. 'She did meet me at Thornton Hall. She came to find out whether Mr Clarence planned to divorce his wife and quizzed me on the subject. I would have told her but I did not want to shame you by revealing you were taking tea with a servant.'

'An ex-servant,' said Sir George. 'Of what were we talking? Ah, yes, the gardens at Thornton Hall. On your next return, Miss Pym, write to me of your arrival and I shall take you to see them.'

'I should like that above all things,' said Hannah, feeling as shy as a girl.

He smiled at her, thinking it was pleasant to squire such a grateful and entertaining lady.

Hannah did not want him to be the first to suggest that they leave, and so she reluctantly gathered up her gloves and reticule.

'Where are you going now?' asked Sir George as they stood outside in Berkeley Square. 'Kensington?'

'Now,' said Hannah. 'I shall go to the Bell Savage in the City and buy a ticket for the Bath coach.'

'Then let me summon a hack for you.'

'I would rather walk, sir,' said Hannah, who was by now so happy and excited that she felt she would burst if she did not get some exercise.

'As you will, Miss Pym. All success and good fortune on your next journey.' He raised his hat and bowed low and Hannah dropped a curtsy. She turned back, however, after a few moments and watched Sir George's tall figure cross Berkeley Square in the dim light and stood there watching for quite a while after he had disappeared from view.

Then Hannah set out for the City. She wanted to jump, to skip, to shout aloud. He had invited her to see the gardens. She could enjoy her next journey without wondering whether he would remember her or would see her at all.

She stood under a street lamp and pulled a folded newspaper cutting from her reticule and studied it. It was an advertisement for the Bath coach.

FLYING MACHINE

As those desirous to pass from London to Bath, or any other Place on their Road, let them repair to the Bell Savage on Ludgate Hill, London, and the White Lion at Bath, at both which places may be received in a Stage Coach every Monday, Wednesday and Friday, which performs the whole journey in Three Days (if God permit) and sets forth at five in the morning.

Passengers to pay one pound five shillings each, who are allowed to carry fourteen Pounds Weight—for all above to pay three halfpence per Pound.

She put it away and set out with a brisker stride towards the City.

Hannah no longer felt lonely. There was so much to look forward to. Lord Harley's wedding, the visit to Thornton Hall gardens, and a whole new adventure on the Bath Road.

The wonderful thing about a stage-coach was that it was a great equalizer. The upper classes, although affecting to despise this mode of travel, often stooped to use it, for a lady, say, could travel with only her maid rather than having to use not only her own carriage but hire five attendants to protect her from the perils of the road.

Hannah finally reached the Bell Savage and purchased an inside ticket for the Bath coach. She stood for a little while afterwards in the bustle of the inn yard. The coach had just arrived from Bath, swinging into the courtyard on its high red wheels. She could smell it, that smell of wood and leather and horse sweat.

Her heart began to beat hard with excitement. She stayed watching and listening for quite a long time before setting out on the long road home. By the time she reached Hyde Park corner, she realized she was tired, but no driver of a hack was going to risk the perils of Knightsbridge Road in darkness and so Hannah forged on alone, nervously looking to right and left, dreading every moment she would be attacked and wondering why she had not gone home immediately after leaving Gunter's.

But at last she wearily climbed the stairs to her rooms above the bakery. She made up the fire and sat down exhausted in a battered armchair and kicked off her shoes.

Her eyes began to droop and once more she felt the swaying of the coach and the long blast of the guard's horn as the Flying Machine bore her through the length and breadth of England.